"FOR DAYS I HAVEN'T BEEN ABLE TO THINK of much else besides you," Mack said. "I need to see you, hold you, kiss you again. I can't seem to stop wanting you, no matter how hard I try."

"Why try at all?" Becky asked, puzzled by his resistance.

"Because I know it's wrong." He leaned closer and kissed one eyelid, then the other, then gave the rim of her ear the same delicious attention.

"Wrong? For a man to want a woman?" she murmured.

He lifted his head and gazed down at her. "In this case, yes. And if you have any sense you'll pack up your picnic basket and hightail it out of here. Now," he added, letting loose a ragged breath.

"Before the Big Bad Wolf eats Little Red Riding Hood?" she teased.

"This isn't a joke, Becky," he said, a melancholy expression on his face.

She reached up and brushed the stubborn lock of hair off his forehead. She'd never felt this strong an attraction for any man, and she wouldn't be scared away. "I'm not going anywhere," she said.

WHAT ARE *LOVESWEPT* ROMANCES?

They are stories of true romance and touching emotion. We believe those two very important ingredients are constants in our highly sensual and very believable stories in the LOVESWEPT line. Our goal is to give you, the reader, stories of consistently high quality that may sometimes make you laugh, sometimes make you cry, but are always fresh and creative and contain many delightful surprises within their pages.

Most romance fans read an enormous number of books. Those they truly love, they keep. Others may be traded with friends and soon forgotten. We hope that each LOVESWEPT romance will be a treasure—a "keeper." We will always try to publish

LOVE STORIES YOU'LL NEVER FORGET
BY AUTHORS YOU'LL ALWAYS REMEMBER

The Editors

Loveswept® 691

IN THE ARMS
OF THE LAW

DEBORAH
HARMSE

BANTAM BOOKS
NEW YORK · TORONTO · LONDON · SYDNEY · AUCKLAND

IN THE ARMS OF THE LAW
A Bantam Book / June 1994

If you would be interested in receiving protective vinyl covers for your
Loveswept books, please write to this address for information:

> Loveswept
> Bantam Books
> P.O. Box 985
> Hicksville, NY 11802

ISBN 0-553-44398-4

Published simultaneously in the United States and Canada

Bantam Books are published by Bantam Books, a division of Bantam Doubleday Dell Publishing Group, Inc. Its trademark, consisting of the words
"Bantam Books" and the portrayal of a rooster, is Registered in U.S. Patent
and Trademark Office and in other countries. Marca Registrada. Bantam
Books, 1540 Broadway, New York, New York 10036.

PRINTED IN THE UNITED STATES OF AMERICA

OPM   0 9 8 7 6 5 4 3 2 1

ONE

Head wounds were invariably bloody.

Detective Mackenzie Hoyle reminded himself of that basic fact a split second after he felt a stream of warm liquid trickle down his forehead. He wiped the back of his hand across his brow, then swore at the bright red blood smeared from his wrist to his knuckles.

"Cripes, what a way to start the day," he muttered, taking two prudent steps back from the shattered schoolroom window before checking for further damage.

Miraculously, his shirt and tie had survived the incident unscathed, as had his black oxfords and charcoal-gray slacks. But the gray herringbone sport coat he'd bought just the week before hadn't been so lucky, he noticed, more than a little ticked off by the splotch of blood on the cuff of the left sleeve. Damn. He'd worn the thing only twice.

"Excuse me, sir. Are you waiting for me?"

Hoyle turned his head in the direction of the voice, and winced at the sharp pain that shot through his neck and down his arm. A dull ache began to pound inside his head. He forced himself to ignore it, instead focusing his attention on the woman standing in the classroom doorway.

He took in the essential details in one glance: Blond hair, blue eyes, an inch or two over five feet, weighing no more than one hundred pounds. The phrase "cute as a button" sprang to mind.

Hoyle drew his brows together into a frown, immediately vowing that if this was Miss Rebekah de Bieren—the teacher he'd come to talk to about his latest murder case—he'd eat his billfold. And the inspector's badge inside.

"Actually," he began, "I was waiting for—"

"Uh-oh," she said, her eyes widening as her gaze swept from the gaping hole in the classroom window, to the rock lying on the floor near his left foot, to the thin line of blood bisecting his forehead. "Looks like someone scored a bull's-eye this time."

"That's one way of putting it," he replied, and allowed himself a more leisurely inspection of the young woman. He was suddenly very curious to know who she was.

Definitely not a teacher, he decided. She looked too young, too hip, too sweet in a girl-next-door sort of way.

Her cheeks were smooth, wrinkle-free, no doubt soft to the touch. Her short hair was stick straight and cut in a jagged fashion that had been popular sometime in the sixties, uneven spikes feathering across her forehead and framing her face in a haphazard way. And her clothes—neon pink-and-yellow parachute pants with matching T-shirt, separated by an extrawide black belt that made her waist look small, *real* small—were about as unteacherish as they could get.

"You know, this never should have happened," she said, shaking her head in obvious disgust as she dumped her armload of books and a red-and-black-plaid thermos on the teacher's desk.

Teacher's desk?

Hoyle muttered a disbelieving expletive and reached for his wallet. Then he remembered that no one had witnessed his impulsive vow to lunch on leather and let his hand fall to his side. Lucky break, he thought, more than a little relieved one of his buddies at the precinct hadn't caught him jumping to conclusions. They'd never let him live it down.

"The taxpayers think they're so clever," she continued as she rummaged through her purse, "voting down education measures year after year. Okay, so they pay less in taxes, have a few more dollars to spend going out to the movies or to dinner at some fancy restaurant. But look who suffers—the poor children, that's who."

Suffering children? Hoyle thought. At the moment, *he* was the one suffering, all because one of those "poor" little buggers had heaved a rock through a school window and clobbered him on the head.

"Whoever threw that rock," she went on, "should be the star pitcher on the school baseball team. But we don't have a baseball team. And do you know why?" she asked, still digging through her handbag.

"No, ma'am, I don't."

"Because we lost our funding for after-school activities a long time ago." She shook her head. "It's a crying shame to waste that kind of talent on mere vandalism, don't you agree, Mr . . . ?"

"Hoyle. *Detective* Hoyle. Santa Ana Police Department."

She jerked her head up and locked her gaze with his. Satisfied he'd finally managed to secure her undivided attention, he reached inside his coat pocket with his clean hand and retrieved his wallet. Using his thumb, he flipped it open and flashed his gold shield. "Homicide Division," he added, taking perverse pleasure in the startled look on her face.

She blinked a couple of times, then drew herself up to her full height. "Homicide?" she repeated. "Your wound must be more serious than I thought."

"Not *that* serious," he replied, silently commending the way she'd recovered her composure so quickly. Still, he didn't laugh at her joke. As far as he was concerned, assault on a police officer—though unintentional—was no laughing matter.

"Well, I'd better take a look." She dug deeper into her purse, came up with a wad of tissues, then rushed over to him. Stretching her arm up, she wiped away some of the blood. "Tip your head down a little, will you?"

Without waiting for him to comply, she pressed on his chin until his eyes were aimed at a pair of white sneakers with neon-yellow laces. She stood on her tiptoes, first brushing his hair away from his forehead, then dabbing at the cut.

Her fingers were warm, her touch soft as a lover's caress. Cupping his face in her hands, she tipped his head to one side, then the other, making hmmmmlike noises as she inspected the damage.

"Typical head wound," she finally stated, sounding somewhat exasperated by her discovery. "Plenty of blood, but when you get right down to it, minimal damage."

He listened to her pronouncement, noticing with interest that one of her hands was now resting on his shoulder. "Are you suggesting I'm hardheaded?" he asked, his mood suddenly lighter than it had been in weeks.

She laughed. "That remains to be seen." Taking hold of his hand, she pulled him toward the door. "Come on, we'd better get you cleaned up."

His attention captured by the slender curve of her hips as she led him briskly down the hall, he followed without protest. One part of his mind took note of the fact that she needed two short steps to every one of his, while the other pondered her strange reaction to the start of her school day.

She'd taken it all in stride—having a rock thrown through her window, the glass littering the floor, his being hurt. He couldn't help wondering if she'd witnessed so many violent situations, she'd gotten used to them. The way he had.

He rejected that notion immediately. In spite of the nothing-rattles-me routine, she had a freshness about her, a sparkling innocence in her clear blue eyes that led him to believe she wasn't as tough as she sounded.

She couldn't possibly be, he told himself, refusing for some reason to even consider that her tough-guy act was no act at all.

"Here we are," she said, pausing in front of a door marked First Aid Room. She pulled a ring of keys out of the pocket of her pants and unlocked the door. Flipping on the light with one hand, she pointed to a bench with the other. "Sit."

Any doubts he'd been clinging to about her being a teacher—or her ability to control a classroom full of kids—vanished. Only teachers gave orders with that kind of authority and expected them to be followed without argument.

Teachers and cops, he amended as he removed his jacket and sat down.

She walked over to the telephone on the wall by the door and dialed a two-digit number. While she waited for someone to pick up on the other end, she paced in the opposite direction as far as the spiral cord would allow.

"Helen," she said a half minute later. "This is Becky. Someone tried to air-condition my civics classroom again this morning. . . . Yes, third time this month. Um-hmm, I know." She glanced at him briefly over her shoulder, her gaze flicking to the cut on his head. "Darned dangerous. Do you think Abe will be able to get the window boarded before school starts?" She looked down at her watch, then ran her hand through her hair. The straight blond strands floated up briefly before drifting back in place around her face. "Thanks. I appreciate it." She hung up the phone, then strode over to the cabinet above the sink.

Hoyle watched her bustle about, gathering speed

as she went along like a hurricane in its prime. She opened cupboard doors and drawers, and in no time she had a full complement of first-aid supplies set out to the right of the sink in a line as straight as a row at roll call in the police academy. Her scrub routine—aided by the use of a soft-bristled brush and steaming hot water—was equally impressive.

Under normal circumstances, he would have felt foolish letting her make such a fuss over what she'd already declared to be nothing more than a simple flesh wound. But thus far, *normal* was the last word he would use to describe anything that had happened since the moment he'd stepped into her classroom.

Besides, he was starting to think that in spite of a brand-new sport coat that was history and a headache that was worthy of the record books, getting beaned in the noggin wasn't so bad after all. Especially since all this quality attention seemed to be included in the deal.

After filling it with water, she set a small stainless steel bowl on the edge of the counter closest to him, then came over to where he sat. He spread his knees wide, and she stepped between his legs, all her concentration focused on the cut on his forehead.

She stood close, so close he could smell her perfume. Testing his ability to name the exact brand, he inhaled deeply. Instantly, his nostrils filled with an unusual scent, something vibrant and alive that suited her to a tee.

A picture of her—naked in a huge bathtub, up to her neck in bubbles—popped into his head. The tempting vision lingered, teasing his imagination with an endless array of erotic possibilities, until he finally, reluctantly, blinked it away.

Finding he was still unable to place the particular scent she was wearing, he concluded he must not have come in contact with it before. He definitely would have remembered it.

Because he had little choice while she tended his wound, he stared straight ahead, his attention immediately drawn to the hollow spot at the base of her throat. He was tempted to reach out and touch the shallow indentation, just to see if her skin was as smooth as it looked. He resisted, and his gaze followed a path of pale freckles downward to where the scoop neck of her T-shirt curved from one collarbone to the other.

"This should only take another minute," she said as she applied disinfectant with a piece of cotton.

Don't hurry on my account, he wanted to say, but wisely kept his mouth shut. He suspected she'd take offense at his smart remark, accuse him of behaving no better than the horny boys in her classes. And she'd be right.

Still, he couldn't seem to stop his thoughts from

wandering into dangerous territory, not as long as she was standing where she was. And certainly not as long as her hip brushed against him each time she twisted to the side to reach for another cotton ball.

He wondered if the kids in her classes had any idea how lucky they were to have her for a teacher. If he'd had Miss de Bieren standing in front of his class when he was in high school twenty years ago, he would have given his best shot at becoming the teacher's pet. And probably would have spent a good deal less time in detention.

"Okay, now for a dressing," she said cheerfully, obviously oblivious to his errant musings.

With one hand holding his hair off his forehead, she leaned closer to him and reached for a bandage, stretching toward the open box on the counter. Before he realized what was happening, she swayed too far to the side and lost her balance.

Instinctively, his hands shot up to her hips to try to prevent her fall. He wasn't quite fast enough.

She fell against him, her right breast skimming across his mouth in deliciously slow motion.

A white-hot blade of desire pierced him, its intensity startling him. Reflexively, his fingers dug into the firm flesh of her fanny, and he sucked in a deep breath, unintentionally drawing in the material of her soft cotton T-shirt as well.

When the oxygen finally reached his brain, he was able to take note of several fascinating facts. One: This day was turning out a whole heck of a lot better than it started; two: The schoolteacher might be a tiny little thing everywhere else, but the part of her nudging his lips wasn't small at all; and three: Her nipple had instantly beaded into a tight knot beneath her shirt, which made him wonder if she was enjoying this little mishap as much as he was.

A definite possibility, he decided, allowing several more pleasure-filled seconds to pass before he convinced himself to set her away from him and back on both feet.

It seemed like a long time before she finally tipped her head down. He looked up at the same moment and found himself staring into a pair of eyes as blue as the uniform shirt he'd worn every day of his life for the first five years he'd been on the force.

Slowly, he lowered his gaze to her lips. They were glossy as glass and pink tinged, like the pink spreading up her neck and over her cheeks. It occurred to him that if he leaned forward and let himself sit an inch taller, his mouth would be even with hers. He'd be able to kiss her.

A voice inside his head warned him he had no business even considering such an action. But he'd spent too much time pondering the scent of her perfume, worked up too great a curiosity about the smoothness of her skin, fantasized too real a picture of her wonderfully naked in a tub full of bubbles. All he wanted was a taste, just one little taste. What could it hurt?

"Sorry," she said. She added a half smile and a nervous giggle to her apology as she took one step back, effectively nixing his experiment. Her hand quivered as she ripped open the bandage she'd managed to snag.

"No problem," he automatically replied, letting his hands fall to his lap as her warm fingers positioned the bandage over his wound and pressed gently against his skin.

No problem? he repeated silently. Then why are you having to use both hands to hide the physical evidence to the contrary? He was as shocked by his unexpected reaction as Miss de Bieren would be—if she discovered it.

And why the hell was he getting so turned on by a pint-size blonde with hardly enough hair to grab hold of? His taste in women usually ran toward long-legged brunettes with lush shoulder-length manes he could sink his hands into.

A one-word explanation came to mind immediately: Overtime. The string of eighteen-hour days he'd been putting in for three straight weeks might be great for his bank account, but it was murder on his social life.

Murder.

Suddenly he remembered what had brought him to Benito Juarez Middle School that morning.

"All done," she said, her tone overly bright as she stepped out from between his legs. She scooped up the handful of soiled cotton balls and tossed them in the wastebasket, then picked up the steel bowl and carried it to the sink. "You'll probably want to take an aspirin or two for pain," she added, her gaze riveted to her hands as she washed and dried them. "I can get you some if you'd like. And I'm really sorry about the accident. As you might have noticed, we've had plenty of rocks thrown through the windows here. But no one's ever been standing in the line of fire before."

"I guess it was just my lucky day," he said quietly. His left hand strayed up to test the damage done to his head, but his eyes watched every move Miss Rebekah de Bieren made.

She was doing it again, he observed, putting on the same nonchalant facade she'd worn in her classroom. Only this time she wasn't pretending to be unaffected by a broken window or the blood streaming down his face. This time, she was trying to convince him she hadn't noticed the sparks that had flashed back and forth between them like lightning in an electrical storm.

Or maybe, he amended, recalling the telltale trembling of her hands a minute earlier, maybe she was trying to convince herself.

TWO

The faculty lounge on the second floor of Benito Juarez Middle School was affectionately referred to as the Bare Bones Break Room. It had one table and three chairs. That was it. No refrigerator, no soda machine, no *coffeepot*—which was the primary reason Becky had brought Detective Hoyle there. She knew she could count on her colleagues to be clustered around the overworked coffee maker in the first-floor lounge this time of day.

Not that she had a burning desire to be alone with this man, she told herself, but if they had police business to discuss, she figured they should do it in private.

Though what she could have to say that would be of interest to a homicide detective, she couldn't imagine.

Once seated, she screwed the cap off her thermos and prayed her hand wouldn't shake as she poured two cups of coffee. She still hadn't recovered from their "close encounter," and though she couldn't say why, she didn't want Detective Hoyle to know how much that little episode had rattled her.

"I hope you don't mind that this has cream and sugar," she said. She handed him the mug she'd retrieved from the bottom drawer of her desk when she'd picked up her thermos on their way to the lounge.

"It could be made with tacks and turpentine and it's be easier to swallow than the stuff they try to pass off as coffee downtown."

She followed his movements as he lifted the mug to his mouth, her gaze drawn to the small cleft in his chin as he blew on the hot coffee. She'd let him use her red mug, the one that had BECKY printed diagonally in bold letters on one side, and an unexpected feeling of intimacy came over her as she watched him drink from the same cup she drank from every morning.

She told herself she should look away before he caught her staring at him. Instead, her gaze remained fixed on his mouth, taking in the sensual fullness of his lower lip, discovering that his upper lip was thinner—but no less sexy—than the bottom one.

Unbidden, the image of her breast brushing

against those very lips sprang into her head. The curious blend of delight and embarrassment she'd felt when she'd fallen against him wasn't far behind.

At the time, she'd wondered if he was enjoying the same delicious head-to-toe tingling she was, maybe even trying to prolong it. He'd sure taken his sweet time about setting her away from him. And for a second there, it had looked like he was about to kiss her.

Get a grip, Beck.

The man was a *cop*, she reminded herself, a little disgusted that she'd allowed her imagination to get away from her.

After all, it was one thing for her to get a thrill out of finding herself in the arms of a handsome officer of the law. It was quite another to think that a man who thrived on danger and who probably lived life on the edge would entertain fantasies about a too-short schoolteacher who hadn't had anything close to a real adventure since she'd finished her two-year tour of duty with the Peace Corps on the Ivory Coast a long time ago.

She sighed and took a sip of coffee from the plastic lid of her thermos. Pretty sure she had both feet firmly planted on terra firma once again, she looked up at him.

"What did you want to talk to me about?" she asked.

Detective Hoyle set down his mug and reached inside his coat pocket to withdraw a small spiral notebook. He flipped past several pages, consulted his notes, then glanced up at her without raising his head.

His eyes were clear and gray, generously framed by brown lashes a couple shades lighter than his cocoa-colored hair. A few gray hairs could be seen on his eyebrows, at his temples, and his neatly trimmed sideburns.

"I spoke to the school principal," he said as he lifted his head and looked her straight in the eyes. "He told me you teach civics."

"Half days, yes. I'm a guidance counselor the rest of the time."

"And Arturo Ramirez is one of your students?"

Arturo. An uneasy feeling crept over her, and she placed the cup on the table in front of her. "Yes, and I'm his counselor, as well. Detective, what's this all about?"

"I think Ramirez might be a key witness in a murder I'm investigating."

His statement sent shock waves bouncing through her, leaving a sense of utter defeat in its wake. Arturo involved in a murder? Had all her efforts to help break the cycle of ignorance and poverty that had plagued his family for generations been wasted?

As fast as it had appeared, the negative notion

evaporated. Becky drew in a breath, said a silent prayer, and summoned the positive attitude that had served her so well when she'd been faced with one seemingly hopeless situation after another on the Ivory Coast.

"I'm sure there must be some mistake," she said in her brightest, most confident voice. "Arturo is my most promising student. He's intelligent, hardworking, eager to learn. He couldn't possibly have anything to do with—"

"Settle down, Miss de Bieren—"

"*Becky*. Call me Becky." Maybe all this talk about Arturo and a murder would feel less threatening if he didn't address her so formally, she reasoned.

"Becky." He nodded politely. "No one is accusing Arturo of murder."

She blew out a relieved breath and realized he was right. The detective had said "witness," not suspect. He probably just wanted to ask Arturo a couple of questions.

"School starts in a few minutes," she told him. "If you want, I can arrange to have Arturo come down to the counseling office so you can—"

"We've already questioned him. He says he doesn't know anything about a body being dumped in the alley behind Main Street last night."

She frowned. "Then why are you here?"

"I was hoping that as his counselor you could

talk some sense into him and get him to tell us the truth."

"What makes you think he hasn't?"

The detective reached for his coffee and took a quick gulp, then shrugged. "They all lie."

"I beg your pardon?"

"Witnesses. They all lie."

She leaned forward. His statement was so outrageous, she had to laugh. "You can't be serious," she said, still smiling.

"On the contrary," he said, his voice flat, devoid of the slightest emotion. "I'm dead serious."

Dead?

Considering the circumstances, Becky wished the detective had chosen a different adjective. And his attitude . . . well, that was even more disturbing. "That's a rather nasty generalization," she said.

"Murder is a nasty business."

"Yes, of course, but that doesn't mean that everyone—"

"With all due respect, ma'am, you're a schoolteacher. Maybe the people you come in contact with tell the truth on occasion, but in my line of work, they never do."

"Never?"

"Nope. The first rule in a homicide investigation," he said, setting down his mug, "is that *everyone* lies. The guy who did the dirty deed lies because he has to. Anyone who might have seen him do it lies because they're afraid, or because they don't want to get involved. And everyone else who's even remotely connected to the case—" He shrugged again. "They lie because they don't have anything better to do than to make my job as difficult as possible."

Becky sat back, ignoring the hollow clicking sound the chair made as her weight shifted to the right rear leg. She watched as the detective swept a hand through his dark brown hair in a frustrated attempt to keep one stray lock in place. That same lock of hair, when dangling down to tickle his forehead, gave him a boyish look that contrasted sharply with the misanthropic opinion he'd just expressed.

He was a good-looking man, she thought, not for the first time. Tall—but who wasn't from her five-feet-two-inch vantage point?—with wide shoulders that filled out his tweed jacket and a broad chest that tapered down to a trim waist. And his legs? Hard as concrete, no exaggeration. Wedged between them while she'd cleaned his cut, she'd felt the incredible strength in his thighs when she'd inadvertently brushed against them while reaching for her supplies. And when she'd fallen, his muscles had tensed, becoming—impossible as it seemed—harder still.

Nice face, nice body, *rotten* attitude. A doggone shame, she thought, but acknowledged that his cynicism was somewhat understandable.

"I guess," she said, "it's not unusual for a man in your position to develop such a negative way of looking at things."

"Ma'am?"

"What I mean is that when a man spends all his time chasing down criminals—"

"Murderers," he corrected her with a smirk. "Not your garden variety criminals."

"Yes, of course." She swallowed hard. "Murderers. But as I was saying, I can see how your job might make you develop a somewhat distrustful approach, but you must realize how damaging that sort of attitude can be. It can eat away at a person and do great damage, both physically and emotionally. You really should try to—"

"Look, I appreciate your concern for my health, but right now I think we should stick to the point."

"But that is the point, don't you see?"

"No, ma'am, but I have a feeling you're going to help me out with that, aren't you?"

Becky made a conscious effort to ignore his sarcastic question, at the same time wondering why she was bothering to try to make this man understand that his pessimistic outlook wasn't doing him any good. Probably because she hated to see people in pain, and if he wasn't in pain right now, he would be eventually. A person couldn't go on like that day after day without doing considerable harm.

"In addition to putting undue stress on your system—which could lead to any number of physical problems," she explained patiently, "I'm afraid you're letting a few negative experiences cloud your judgment."

He quirked one gray-tinged brow. "A few? Lady, I've been a cop for sixteen years—with the Homicide Division for the last seven—and I've had a hell of a lot more than a 'few negative experiences,' as you so delicately put it. And if it weren't for that 'cloudy judgment' of mine, I'd have had my head blown off my shoulders more times than I care to remember."

"Well . . . in this case," she said emphatically, determined not to be intimidated, "I'd have to say you're wrong. I know Arturo quite well. I've been his counselor since he was in sixth grade, and this year, he's the top student in my eighth grade civics class. He's a good kid."

The detective leaned forward and rested his elbows on his knees, clasping his hands together in front of him. He smiled at her. It wasn't much of a smile, just the hint of one actually, but she realized it was the first time he'd let one slip out. She had no doubt he'd be horrified to know it made him look downright friendly.

"Miss de Bieren—Becky," he amended when she opened her mouth to correct him. "It's clear to me that you're a kind, warmhearted, generous sort of person."

She straightened. "Why, yes. I am."

"I'll bet you pick up stray cats off the street, buy Girl Scout cookies from every little girl who knocks on your front door, send donations to half a dozen soup kitchens so the homeless will be sure to have Thanksgiving dinner."

He hadn't mentioned her work as a volunteer one evening a week at the hospital, or the fact that she participated in an annual walkathon to raise money to help fight childhood diseases. But then, she took part in so many worthwhile causes, he couldn't possibly have named them all.

Or want to, she decided as his sarcastic tone finally hit her. "You don't have to make it sound like I'm a soft touch just because I help others."

"Sorry. I didn't mean it that way."

She folded her arms in front of her, not at all sure his apology was sincere. "I try to be a good citizen."

"Yes, ma'am, and that's exactly what I'm asking you to be now—a good citizen. I'm conducting a serious police investigation today, and so far, I don't have much to go on. If you could just talk to Arturo, try to make him understand that it's in his best interests to tell the police what he knows."

"He already told you he doesn't know anything. Why can't you believe that?"

Hoyle stood up so fast, his chair slid back and tipped over, hitting the cracked linoleum floor with a loud thud. He turned away, then whipped back around to face her. For a moment, he simply stared at her. Then he leaned over, planted one hand on the table, and gripped the back of her chair with the other, effectively trapping her in her seat.

His face was so close to hers, she could smell his tangy after-shave, count the individual lashes surrounding his cold gray eyes.

"I'll give you three good reasons why I don't believe Arturo," he said in a soft voice that clashed with the harsh look on his face. "One, I've got a dead man with his throat slashed clear through to the back of his neck. Two, I've got a liquor store owner who says Arturo rides right past the empty lot where the body was found every night after the boy finishes restocking the beer and wine cooler. And three, I've got an hysterical mother who tells me her son was all shook up when he came home last night and she's scared to death he's in some kind of trouble." He took a deep breath, then moved in closer still. "*That's* why I think your intelligent, hardworking, eager-to-learn 'good kid' is holding out on me."

Becky held her breath. "Why didn't you tell me all this earlier?" she whispered, trying with all her might not to conjure up the bloody image he'd described in such graphic detail.

"Because my job is to *get* information out of people, not give it away," he shouted, his nose almost touching hers.

Startled by his angry outburst, she leaned away from him as far as the back of the chair would allow. Her eyes were riveted to the vein that traveled from the edge of his right eyebrow to his hairline. It was throbbing.

"Well," she said weakly. "I guess that makes sense."

"So glad you think so," he said between clenched teeth, then straightened and backed away from her.

He stood motionless, head down, hands in tight balls at his hips, for several minutes, no doubt trying to get his temper under control. Gradually, his shoulders relaxed. His fists unclenched. Another minute crept by and the blue vein on his forehead ceased its pounding. When he finally raised his head, he looked relatively calm, except for the way he held his mouth in a tight, thin line, as though he had to clamp down on his lips to keep from losing control again.

She was sorry her defense of Arturo had infuriated him and made it appear as though she was unwilling to cooperate. Obviously he was under a tremendous amount of pressure to solve this case, and from what he'd already told her, he wasn't having much luck. That would explain why he was so short tempered.

"It must be very difficult being a police officer," she said quietly. She continued, ignoring the look of utter disbelief on his face. "And I truly sympathize with the tough job you have to do. But I think I should warn you that yelling at people and bullying them is not the way to get them to cooperate."

"What? Oh, for crying out loud—" He looked away briefly. "Are you for real?"

"What I mean," she went on, refusing to let him ruffle her, "is that if you lost your temper like this with Arturo, it wouldn't surprise me if he was reluctant to tell you what he knows. These kids don't think much of the police to start with, you know."

Hoyle walked over and sat back down. He scooted his chair closer to hers, then leaned forward, again resting his elbows on his thighs as he clasped his hands together. "You think you might be able to do better with the kid?"

"Certainly," she blurted out, then realized she'd just allowed him to goad her into doing what he'd asked her to do in the first place—convince Arturo to cooperate with the police.

"Great. Then get him in here. Now."

Becky sighed. She had no great desire to upset him further, but she had no choice. "That won't work."

"Why not?"

"Because he already told you he didn't see anything. If I come right out and ask him about last night, it'll look like I don't believe him, and that's as good as calling him a liar."

"He is a liar."

She gave him a disapproving scowl. "What happened to innocent until proven guilty?"

He frowned, then crossed his arms over his chest. "If you can't ask him about it," he said, ignoring her question, "how do you suggest we get him to talk?"

She thought about it for a minute. "Maybe I could try to find a way to bring up the subject in our counseling session."

He looked at her hard, as if he was assessing the plan she'd come up with, then stood. "I suppose it's worth a try. When is your session?"

"Tomorrow afternoon."

He shook his head. "Won't work."

"Sure it will. The appointment is already scheduled. You couldn't ask for a more perfect time to—"

"Look," he said, cutting her short in a voice that suggested he was using the last scrap of patience he possessed. "The first twenty-four hours after a murder is committed are crucial to the success of the investigation, and I don't have time to waste waiting around for the *perfect* time for you and Arturo to have your powwow. You got that?"

Becky felt her temper flare. "Rule number one," she began, even as she wondered why she let his smart remarks get to her so easily, "everyone lies. Rule number two, every second counts. How am I doing?"

He tipped his head to one side. "You're catching on."

"Think there's a chance I'll get a passing mark in Rules of Homicide 101?" She was surprised to hear the wisecrack come from her mouth this time. Her students were always smarting off, but she never allowed herself to be goaded into responding in kind.

The detective startled her once again by reaching down and wrapping his hands around her arms. Slowly, he brought her to her feet, drawing her closer and closer until there was hardly more than an inch of space between their bodies.

"If you really want a good grade, little girl," he said, his voice soft and smooth and full of seductive promise, "you might try buttering up the teacher."

Becky inched up onto her toes and rested her hands on his shoulders. Her lips curved into a challenging smile. She knew she was playing with fire, and this man appeared to be a pyrotechnic wizard. But she was tired of being bullied and yelled at and coerced into cooperating. She was tired of being made to feel foolish because she didn't know the first thing about investigating a murder.

Most of all, she was tired of being thought of as a "little girl."

She was a woman, a twenty-eight-year-old woman, and it was about time the detective became aware of that fact.

"With this particular instructor," she said, matching his suggestive tone with one that was equally provocative, "I'm not sure it's possible to get on his good side."

He winked. "Believe me, it's possible."

"Do you suppose you could give me a few tips?"

His hands dropped to her hips as he smiled. "You were on the right track when you were cleaning my cut."

Remembering the heat that brief embrace had generated, and feeling as though his hands were searing straight through her clothes to her skin, Becky realized she was about to get more than she'd bargained for. She had to do something quickly to douse the fire she'd started.

She let her hands fall to her sides and took several steps back, forcing him to release her and putting some much-needed distance between them.

"Well . . . actually," she managed to say, "traditional methods have always worked best for me. I think I'll stick with the shiny-red-apple-for-the-teacher routine."

He quirked one brow and gave her a look the

devil himself would have admired. "So . . . you're into forbidden fruit too?"

"Wrong lesson book, Professor Hoyle," she said, forcing herself to smile so he'd get the impression she thought he was just making a joke. The truth was, his words conjured up all sorts of naughty visions, none of which were the least bit funny.

"That's okay," he said. "I have a better idea anyway."

Bending her head down, she put one hand over her mouth to hide her smile. It pleased her to no end to know he really did see her as a woman. He must, or he wouldn't bother to play this outrageous game with her.

"I'll bet you have a whole lot of ideas," she murmured, eager to hear his next shameless comment.

"How about you come up with a halfway decent plan to get Arturo to tell me what he saw last night?"

Her head shot up. She let out a weary sigh, realizing he'd gotten the better of her again. He'd teased her with seductive looks, coaxed her along with suggestive phrases—then unceremoniously dumped a bucket of ice-cold water over her head to bring her back down to earth. With effort, she pretended not to be bothered by the abrupt end to their game. Or by the fact that she'd been trounced by a master gamesman.

"I suppose there must be some way to find out

if he knows anything without coming right out and saying it."

"I'm all ears," he said.

Running her fingers through her hair in frustration, she began to pace the length of the small room, trying to think of how to reach Arturo. A minute later, she jerked to a halt, whirling around to face the detective.

"Hey, I've got it. I'll make civic responsibility the subject of my lesson in civics class today. We can talk about how a person can do their part to keep the streets in their neighborhood safe, and how they should come forward if they have any information that would help the police solve a crime. Maybe Arturo will decide to—"

"Oh, cripes. You don't honestly believe that will work?"

She crossed her arms in front of her. "It might."

His expression remained disbelieving. "I don't care how good your little lesson might be, those kids would rather eat dirt than cooperate with a cop."

Becky frowned. He was right, of course, but there was no way she'd admit that to him now. He'd scored too many points in their last match for her to concede this one without putting up a good fight.

Besides, he could get as sarcastic as he wanted about her inexperience with homicide investigations, but if he thought he could get away with questioning her ability as a teacher, he had another think coming.

Furthermore, this was the only plan she could conceive on the spur of the moment, and the detective had made it clear she didn't have all day to come up with one that had a better chance of succeeding.

Trying to look more confident about her impromptu idea than she felt, she folded her hands in front of her and looked him straight in the eye.

"We'll see, Detective," she said, coolly. "We'll see."

Hoyle took the long route back to the station house so he could swing by and take another look at the crime scene—such as it was—in the light of day.

He remembered that a car dealership had once occupied the corner lot, but after they'd moved to the giant auto park in Tustin, the showroom and service buildings had been demolished.

The property belonged to the city now and was nothing more than an empty lot filled with brick and concrete rubble, interspersed with foot-high weeds and surrounded by a wobbly chain-link fence that did a poor job of keeping trespassers out. He squeezed through an opening on the south side of the lot and walked to the center.

Just as he'd thought, it was a wasted trip. He couldn't find so much as a hint of the chalk the medical examiner had used to outline the victim's body, thanks to the steady rain that had kept up most of the previous night.

Lousy luck, breaking a record-setting period of drought on the night of a homicide. Worse yet, he had not one, but *two* possible witnesses, and both were about as talkative as the dead man.

Hands in his pockets, he stared down at the spot where the victim's feet had been. He couldn't help thinking that what this investigation needed most was a lucky break. So far, it had been nothing but one damned headache after another.

Frowning, he raised his hand to his head and patted his bandage. Yeah, he had a whopper of a headache, all right. Worse yet, he was frustrated.

Frustrated by a naive schoolteacher who was foolish enough to believe a student of hers was telling the truth when *he* knew damn well the kid was lying through his teeth. Frustrated because the little lesson plan she'd cooked up to inspire the kid to come forward and do his civic duty didn't have one chance in a million of succeeding.

And he was frustrated, dammit, because standing there in the middle of a vacant lot that stank to the heavens of rotting garbage and broken wine bottles, he still had no trouble recalling the intriguing scent of the schoolteacher's perfume.

THREE

Becky spotted Hoyle as soon as she stepped out the rear exit of the school.

Leaning against the driver's side door of her car, arms folded in front of him, feet crossed at the ankles, he looked relaxed, more like an easygoing lover patiently waiting for his sweetheart than a Type-A homicide detective racing against the clock to catch a murderer.

The casual stance had something to do with it, of course, but the real reason he looked so appealing was because he was treating her to what she'd come to think of as one of his rare smiles—mouth turned up at both corners and everything. *That* made him look friendly. And not just good-looking, as she'd first thought when they'd been sitting together in the teachers' lounge that morning, but downright sexy.

Still, she wasn't for one moment fooled into thinking he was paying a social call. Detective Hoyle was there because he was itching to know if her plan to get Arturo to come forward had worked.

Reluctantly, she walked toward him. "Why, Detective Hoyle," she said, hoping to put off confessing her failure for a few minutes longer. "What a pleasant surprise."

Hoyle noted that Becky's smile was as insincere as her overly cheerful greeting, and he almost laughed out loud. He'd bet dollars to donuts she was disappointed to find him waiting for her, which meant her efforts with Arturo had been no more successful than he'd thought they'd be. For once he had hoped he'd lost a bet.

"It's nice to see you again, as well," he replied. Unlike her, he meant it, and not just because she might well be his only hope of solving what had become—as of a few hours ago—a double homicide.

"How'd you know this was my car?" she asked.

He glanced around at an array of dull-looking sedans and practical minivans, then down at her car. It was a two-door number, a compact sporty model with a white convertible top and a sunshine-yellow paint job that seemed to vibrate with energy. Just the way she did.

"No, let me guess," she continued without giving him a chance to reply. "You flashed your badge at some poor hardworking state employee at the Department of Motor Vehicles and ordered her to fork over any and all information about said vehicle."

Hoyle answered with a noncommittal shrug, deciding to let her think he'd gone to all that trouble to find out what he had, in fact, known from the moment he'd driven into the lot.

"Nice bit of detective work, Officer, but using inside sources could be considered cheating. School-teachers," she added, drawing her brows together into the least intimidating scowl he'd ever seen, "frown on cheating."

"Caught in the act," he said, holding his hands in the air as if she had a standard issue 9mm Glock trained on his heart. Come to think of it, he mused, maybe she did have some weapon he should fear. Look at how his heart had started to pound the moment he'd seen her step from the back door of the school. He wanted to still be angry with her—and her ridiculously naive approach to life—but he couldn't manage it. That worried him. He shook off his anxiety and narrowed his gaze. "What's my punishment, Teach?"

Becky laughed at his mock-serious pose and wondered how much time he'd had to spend in detention for making smart remarks to his teachers. Plenty, she decided. But in spite of being a handful to discipline, he would have been exactly the type of student she enjoyed having in her classes—intelligent, quick-thinking, the kind who kept you on your toes every minute. Those were the ones who provided the most interesting challenges—and the biggest rewards.

She nodded toward the bandage on his forehead. "Looks like you served your sentence in advance. How's the head?"

"Hard as ever. How'd the lesson go?"

She bit back a groan a split second before it slipped out of her mouth, and reminded herself she shouldn't be surprised he'd wasted no time getting to the point. His time-is-of-the-essence philosophy had come through loud and clear when they'd spoken earlier.

"Let's see," she said, determined to direct the conversation away from Arturo and her ill-fated lesson for as long as possible. "I only had to dodge one paper airplane, and Calvin Lester didn't snore this time when he fell asleep. So all in all, I'd say the lesson went pretty well."

"Did Ramirez take the bait?"

"Bait? Please, Detective, we're discussing one of my students, not red snapper."

Hoyle forced himself to take a deep breath. "Did Arturo talk to you about where he was last night?"

He watched Becky tip her head back and look up into the sky. She appeared to be following the progress of a cumulus cloud as it floated on by, but as far as he was concerned, she was stalling. "Miss de Bieren?" he prodded.

She pulled her gaze away from the puffy clouds. "No, he didn't."

Hoyle studied her as she fidgeted with her load of books and papers, straightening the stack in her arms as if it were important they be lined up just so. Then she glanced down at the pavement and kicked a pebble out of the way before adjusting the shoulder strap on her purse—several times.

She didn't look at him. Not once.

She was hiding something, he decided. Maybe Arturo hadn't come right out and told her all about his eventful evening, but he'd said *something*.

He wasn't surprised that she was holding out on him. She no doubt considered it her duty to protect the kid. Well, he had a duty, as well—to solve this case.

"He did show up for class, though, didn't he?" he asked, mentally searching through his bag of tricks to come up with a way to get her to tell him the unedited truth.

She finally looked up at him. "Certainly."

"Did he seem nervous? Fidgety? Anxious to get out of there?"

She pursed her lips and drew her features into a thoughtful expression. "No, not really."

"Well then, did he appear to be distracted? Or did he do something that might indicate he had something on his mind? Something *important*, maybe?"

She chuckled. "Hardly. He fell asleep."

"What?"

"I said he—"

"I heard you!" he shouted. "Why didn't you tell me that right away?"

"Because it didn't seem important," she said, clutching her books tighter, pressing them against her chest. "And I don't know what you're getting all upset about anyway. He dozed off for a few minutes, that's all. Besides, that sort of thing isn't all that unusual in this school. Lots of students have evening jobs to help make ends meet at home and they don't always get a full night's sleep."

Hoyle took a deep breath and told himself to calm down. Shouting wasn't the way to get the answers he needed, as she'd pointed out so eloquently that morning.

"What about Arturo?" he asked, relieved to hear his voice was back down to conversation volume. "Does he catnap often?"

"Oh, no. This is the first time. Like I told before, he's an excellent student. But that might explain it," she added with a shrug. "Maybe he stayed up too late because he was studying for a test."

Years of experience of hiding his true feelings from suspects and witnesses allowed Hoyle to maintain a neutral expression on his face, but it was a struggle.

She was so naive, so *damn* naive, she believed Arturo had pulled an all-nighter to study for a test.

No way. Hoyle would bet a round of drinks at Crazy Jack's Bar and Grill that the reason the kid was so darned tuckered out today was because he'd stayed awake worrying about the scene he'd witnessed on his way home from the liquor store—and about what would happen to him when the cops found out he'd told a bald-faced lie when he'd said he "didn't see nothin'."

Hoyle looked at Becky, then shook his head, wondering how anyone could be so innocent, so . . . gullible.

But she was. And while he had a hard time grasping such naïveté, he nevertheless found it refreshing to run across someone who sincerely believed people had honest, straightforward reasons for everything they said and did. Hell, she probably believed in the tooth fairy too.

It was a damn shame he had to burst her bubble.

He straightened, pushing himself away from her car. He didn't particularly like what he was about to do, but he was willing to take advantage of her unsuspecting nature if it would shake her up enough so that she'd tell him what had really happened with Arturo that morning.

"Well, thanks anyway for all you've done."

She reached into her purse and withdrew her keys. "You're welcome, but . . . is that it? That's all you want to know?"

"Yes, ma'am. And I appreciate the way you've tried to help. Not many people are so willing to cooperate with the police nowadays."

"That's a shame." She looked truly unhappy about the situation too.

He shrugged. "I guess they don't care enough to get involved." He turned and started to walk away, then stopped abruptly and whipped around. "Listen, I don't suppose you'd like to go get a cup of coffee or something, would you?"

Becky blinked, his invitation taking her by complete surprise. "Me?"

He shot a suspicious glance around the parking lot, then gave her a mock-serious look. "You see anyone else I might be talking to here?" he asked, and pretended to check for someone hiding beneath her car.

She laughed, thinking this was a side of the detective she never would have guessed existed—a silly side that showed he didn't always take things so seriously. Maybe there was hope for the man after all, she thought, wanting to believe he wasn't a hard-hearted cynic through and through.

Wasting no time, she unlocked her car door and stashed her stuff inside before closing it tight again. "Let's go, Officer."

Hoyle took her arm and led her to his car. "The only thing is," he said, "I have to go talk to this woman about a case first. It shouldn't take long. Only a minute or two."

Becky walked slowly back to the car, leaving Hoyle to finish up his interview with Mrs. Denton, the woman they'd come to see. She crossed her arms and leaned them on the roof of the unmarked police sedan, letting her head drop until her chin rested on her forearms.

In the background, she could hear the detective telling Mrs. Denton to call him if she remembered anything that might help him in his efforts to catch the man who'd murdered her husband.

The Dentons' baby's cries faded, and Becky heard the apartment door bang shut, then the sound of foot-steps growing louder as Hoyle approached the car.

"Are you all right?" he asked.

"How will she manage?" she asked without look-ing up at him.

"I don't know."

She raised her head, her gaze falling on the faded rust-colored paint peeling off the door of the apartment directly across the street. Similar to the one they'd just come out of, the building had a wooden porch that sagged in the middle, and a battered aluminum rain gutter that hung off one end of the roof and dragged on the weed-infested front lawn. She squeezed her eyes shut, willing herself not to cry, knowing in her heart that every time she thought about that family she would have to fight back tears.

"She has three small children and another on the way. How will she pay her rent?" Her voice cracked. She took a deep breath. "How will she put food on the table, buy clothes for everyone?"

"It'll be rough. If she's lucky, she'll qualify for some government assistance and get by."

"What if she isn't *lucky*?" she asked him, opening her eyes in time to see a skinny gray cat dash across the street seconds before a car roared by. "Do they join the swelling ranks of homeless families forced to live on the streets, find their meals in restaurant trash bins, huddle together at night in a cardboard box because they have no other way to keep warm? What in heaven's name are they going to *do*?"

Hoyle heard her passionate plea and knew she was expecting him to give her some kind of answer. He didn't have one, of course. Not one she'd want to hear. Rotten things happened every day, he could have told her. A ruthless way of looking at it, but it was the truth.

Life was unfair.

And frankly, it wasn't his job to sugarcoat that well-known axiom in order to make it palatable for the "Little Miss Sunshines" of the world. No one had done that for him when he'd needed it a few years ago, and he was inclined to think he'd been better off in the long run. No illusions, no disappointments.

That didn't mean he was completely coldhearted, though. He felt bad about the miserable future in store for that lady and her kids. Still, he couldn't do a damn thing about it.

His patience finally spent, he opened his mouth to tell the schoolteacher just when she turned to face him. His urge to teach her a long overdue lesson in reality vanished.

She was pale, not a hint of the pink-tinged fresh-ness he'd found so charming when she'd blushed in the First Aid Room that morning, and her beautiful blue eyes were brimming with unshed tears. She bit down on her bottom lip, then blinked, and the tears she'd been holding back broke loose and spilled down her cheeks.

"Ah, c'mon, don't do that," he said, feeling more than a little frustrated by this surprising turn of events.

He'd been prepared for just about any type of reaction from Denton's widow. Murder victims' next of kin had been known to faint, wail uncontrollably. Hell, he'd even had them call him every dirty name in the book and blame *him* for the victim's death.

But that woman hadn't shed a tear. Not one. He had to hand it to her—she was tough.

The schoolteacher, he realized, suddenly seeing what should have been clear to him all along, was not. She felt too deeply, cared too much.

The way she acted, he'd thought she could handle just about anything—the repeated vandalism in her classroom, blood dripping down a strange man's face.

And her performance in front of Mrs. Denton? Worthy of an Academy Award. She'd been a tower of strength and compassion when the woman had needed it the most.

It was all a sham.

Miss Rebekah call-me-Becky de Bieren wasn't a Rock of Gibraltar at all. She was more like a Campfire Marshmallow. Soft, melt-in-your-mouth sweet, remarkably easy to chew up and swallow.

Which is exactly what you did, you jerk, he told himself as he watched the tears roll down her face.

She was an innocent, one of a rare class of humans that steadfastly clung to the belief that people were inherently decent and honest. She didn't have an ounce of malice in her body, and he'd cruelly subjected her to the cold, hard facts of life—when he should have tried his best to protect her from them.

As he watched one fat tear trickle down her cheek, he told himself he should do the smart thing—apologize for being an idiot, take her back to her car, and see her safely home. Then he'd drive away without looking back and forget everything that had happened in the last hour.

Instead, he reached out and took her face in his hands, his thumbs skimming over soft cheeks and damp lashes. He swiped at the drops as fast as they fell, irrationally convincing himself that if he spread them around until they disappeared, he could forget they'd ever existed in the first place.

Still, as quickly as he rubbed one tear away, another took its place, until he'd wiped away a river of hurt so deep and wide, it tore a ragged path through his unguarded heart.

Without thinking, he put his arms around her and gathered her to him, hoping that by holding her close, he could somehow stanch the flow of pain. She wrapped her arms around his waist and held on tight, shaking, mumbling words into his shirt he couldn't quite make out.

Instinctively, he tightened his hold on her, rubbing his hands up and down her back, trying his damnedest to absorb the hurt he'd caused. She continued to cry softly, and he wracked his brain for something he could try—anything at all—that might make her stop crying. Finally, he decided he'd have to confess his sin, tell her the real reason he'd brought her there, and hope that by coming clean with her, he might somehow fix things.

He gripped her shoulders and pushed her away from him so he could look straight at her when he told her the truth about Denton.

What he saw when he looked into her eyes nearly brought him to his knees. He saw compassion, as if *he* were the one who needed comforting.

"It must be awful for you," she said, her voice catching when she tried to talk.

"Me?" He wasn't imagining it, he realized. She really did feel sorry for *him*.

She nodded, and wiped her cheek with the back of her hand. "You're a homicide detective. You see this sort of situation all the time."

He nodded slowly. "Yeah, I guess I do."

"Well, it must be very hard to face people who've lost loved ones, people like Mrs. Denton"—she glanced at the apartment they'd just come out of—"knowing they're having such a horrible time of it and that you can't help them."

Hoyle didn't know what to say. Now that he'd realized what a soft touch she was, he'd pretty much expected her to read him the riot act for *not* doing something to help that poor woman. She didn't, though. She seemed to understand—and empathize with—the difficult position he found himself in all too often. He shook his head, hardly able to believe that after what he'd done to her, she still managed to scrape up sympathy for the pathetic bastard who'd made her cry. Shaking his head again, he decided she was nothing short of amazing. And way too good for the likes of him.

His hands slowly glided over her narrow shoulders and up her neck, then kept going until he cupped the back of her head. He let his thumbs caress her cheekbones, lost his fingers in hair that was as soft as feathers and impossible to tame.

You're making a big mistake, a voice inside his head warned. But he was beyond listening to reason.

Gazing down into blue eyes glistening with tears, he paused. None of this made sense anyway, he told himself, this strong attraction he felt toward a woman who wasn't even his type. And it was a sure bet he wasn't hers, either.

No, it didn't make sense, especially when he had a job to do and she was part of that job. But he was holding her and she was letting him, and for the moment, nothing else seemed important.

With his thumbs he applied just enough pressure

on her chin to tip her head back until her lips were positioned just so. He bent forward until her mouth was close, almost as close as it had been in the First Aid Room, when he'd wanted to kiss her. When he'd wanted just a taste.

This time he had no intention of letting the opportunity slip by him. And he seriously doubted a taste would be enough.

FOUR

Becky stared up at Hoyle through eyes blurred by tears, fascinated by what she saw.

His pupils were suddenly jet black and as mysterious as an unexplored cave, and the clear gray surrounding them had turned a smoky hue that brought to mind stormy nights and slow-burning fires. A feeling of excitement—at once thrilling and a bit frightening—skittered down her spine and did funny things to her insides.

This time, she decided without a moment of doubt, the look in his eyes wasn't a product of her overactive imagination. Neither was it a sneaky tactic used to underscore a suggestive remark.

This time it was the genuine article, desire with a capital *D*, and this time, he really was going to kiss her.

Later, when she was alone in the quiet of her own apartment, she'd try to figure out why she felt such a strong attraction to a man who was cynical, sarcastic, and, at times, downright annoying. But for now, she simply acted.

She placed her hands on his shoulders and raised onto her toes as she tipped her head to one side. His warm breath mingled with her own as his mouth hovered over hers. She shuddered with anticipation, at the same time frustrated by the quarter inch that still separated them.

Dear God, she prayed, *for just one second, could you please let me be taller?* An instant later, her prayer was answered.

Hoyle cupped her face in his hands as his lips brushed against hers, once, twice, then a third time, delivering kisses that were sweet and gentle, kisses so tantalizingly brief, they left her aching for more.

Was this some sort of taste test, she wondered, a chance for him to discover if he liked what she had to offer? Or was it a cautious experiment, a way for him to find out if she was willing to give what he wanted to take?

Before she could decide, his mouth captured hers, taking possession with a force that stunned her, leaving no doubt in her mind about what he was trying to tell her. He wanted more, and he didn't mind doing whatever it took to convince her that she wanted the same.

She leaned into him, pressing her body closer to his, telling him as plainly as she knew how that she didn't need convincing; and telling herself, in a way she couldn't ignore, that it had been way too long since she'd allowed herself the mind-numbing experience of simple, straightforward, honest-beyond-belief passion. It felt good, so good she didn't want it to stop. Ever.

She slid her hands down between their bodies and rested her palms flat against his chest. His heart pounded beneath her fingertips, each beat coming harder and faster than the one before in a steady rhythm she would have sworn matched the throb of her own heartbeat.

His thumbs caressed her cheeks as his teeth gently nibbled at the corner of her mouth. Then he drew her bottom lip into his mouth, running his tongue around the edges, tasting, teasing for what seemed like hours, before finally releasing it and taking her entire mouth with his in another punishingly tender attack.

One minute he was sweet and gentle, the next hard and demanding. She never knew what to expect— except more bone-melting pleasure.

She parted her lips to take in some air. His tongue plunged into her mouth, surprising her yet again, stealing her breath and leaving her weak.

And then it was over.

He raised his head and gazed down at her as they each took in huge gulps of air. The look on his face told her he was astounded by the intensity of what had just happened between them.

So was she, and suddenly she felt depleted, physically and emotionally tapped out. The meeting with the widow and the tears she'd allowed herself to shed for the first time in a very long while had drained her of most of her energy. The passion she'd given free rein to with a man she hardly knew had siphoned off the rest.

She gripped the lapels of his tweed jacket, certain that if she let go she'd either sink to the ground in a boneless heap, or float into the sky like a hot-air balloon cut loose from its tether.

As if sensing her need, he gathered her close and let her lean on him, rubbing her back as he whispered soothing words. He kissed one eyelid, then the other, and in doing so, somehow gave her the strength she needed to blot out the heartbreaking picture in her mind of the widow and her children. His lips brushed against the outer rim of her ear, and she was able to banish the gut-wrenching cries of the Denton baby from her memory as well.

She rested her head against his chest and sighed. How odd it felt to let someone else be strong for a change, to be the one comforted, instead of doing the comforting. And how odd it was that it had happened with this stranger, a man whose outlook on life and attitude toward people was so different from her own. It felt right, though, to be standing there in his arms, maybe because he no longer seemed like a stranger.

When her breathing finally returned to normal, she lifted her head and looked up at him. Now that she felt better, her tearful outburst seemed foolish. She wiped away the last of her tears and smiled shyly.

"I don't usually fall apart like that," she said. "I'm sor—"

"Shh." He touched his fingers to her lips. "I'm the one who should be apologizing."

"For what?" She thought for a moment, then her eyes widened. "Oh—you don't mean because you kissed me, do you? Because if that's why you think you should apologize, you're wrong. I wanted it as much as you did."

He gave her a shocked look, then burst out laughing. "Are you always this honest?"

"Of course. Why wouldn't I be?"

Hoyle saw the sincere look on her face and wanted to kick himself for asking such a dumb question. And for laughing.

Of course she was always that honest, and she expected that everyone else was as well. Which was exactly why he'd managed to get away with the stunt he'd just pulled—because she'd never suspect him of having an ulterior motive for bringing her to see the widow in the first place.

And that brought him back to the confession he'd been about to make before he'd gotten sidetracked by compassionate blue eyes and a mouth that seemed to be made for kissing.

"No, I'm not sorry I kissed you, Becky, but I never should have—"

"Never should have? Oh, no." She pushed against him, but he didn't loosen his hold on her. "You're married, aren't you?" She buried her face in her hands. "Oh, this is awful."

He put his finger under her chin and brought her head up. "Look at me, Beck." She opened her eyes. "I am not married. I'm not even involved with anyone right now." She looked so relieved, he had to chuckle. Then his smile faded. "But I never should have brought you here. It was a big mistake."

"What kind of mistake?"

He looked away. "Damn, I don't know how to tell you this."

An uneasy feeling settled in the pit of her stomach. "Tell me what, Detect—"

"Please, can't you call me Mack? After all, we're not exactly strangers anymore, are we?"

Becky felt her face grow warm and knew she was turning a bright shade of pink. It was embarrassing to think she'd let herself get so carried away with the man. She'd only met him that morning. She drew in a breath and waited for the warmth in her cheeks to subside. "Okay, Mack. Will you please tell me what you're talking about?"

"I'm talking about this." He waved one arm in the direction of the apartment they'd come out of a few minutes ago, but she had a feeling he meant more than just the building. "I never intended to make you cry. I just wanted to know what really happened when you talked to Arturo today."

"Arturo? What does he have to do with the Dentons?"

Mack closed his eyes briefly. "We brought Arturo and Frank Denton—that woman's husband—downtown for questioning last night because we had reason to believe one or both might have information about the homicide."

"But I thought—" She turned her head to look at the apartment. "I thought Mrs. Denton's husband was the one who was murdered last night."

"No, twenty-four hours ago he was just another possible witness to that murder, but he insisted he hadn't seen anything—just like Arturo." He brought his hands up and cupped the back of her head, forcing her to look straight at him. "But this afternoon we found him with his throat slashed open. Do you know what that means?"

Becky opened her mouth to speak but no words came out. She shook her head.

"It means someone is willing to go to any lengths to see that no one talks to the police about what they saw last night."

She stepped back, breaking his hold on her. Suddenly feeling very cold, she hugged her arms around herself. Something strange was going on here, she thought, wondering how they'd managed to go from kissing to discussing murder in a matter of seconds.

"Why did you bring me here?" she asked. She glanced at her surroundings, taking in the cracked concrete, the foot-high weeds, the stripped and abandoned car parked across the street, before bringing her gaze back to his. "I thought we were going to go get a cup of coffee."

"After my appointment."

"Right, but you didn't tell me your appointment had something to do with a murder. Or that Arturo was involved."

"Because I wanted to catch you off guard. I thought if you came face-to-face with this woman and got a good look at what happened when her husband wouldn't cooperate with us, you'd be so scared that the same thing could happen to Arturo, you'd open up and tell me what really went on with him in school today."

She took another step back. "You let me think

this was just a casual invitation to go have coffee after your 'appointment,' when all along it was part of some plan to upset me?"

He looked away again. "Basically, yes."

"You *tricked* me."

"I needed to—"

"And you used that woman and her kids."

"Well . . . yes, but—"

"This is amazing." She shook her head several times. "Now I understand why you're so sure everyone lies."

"Now wait just a minute. I never lied to you."

"Maybe not in so many words, but you didn't tell me the truth either."

"I was only trying to do my job."

"Your job? I trusted you. I thought you asked me to go get a cup of coffee with you because you liked me, when all along—"

"Becky, will you let me explain—"

"It was just a trick."

"If you'll listen for one minute—"

"And you *kissed* me."

She hated to admit it—even to herself—but that was what hurt the most. She'd thought he'd wanted her, *desired* her, when all he'd really wanted was information about Arturo. Without saying another word to him, she turned and headed up the street.

"Hey, where the hell do you think you're going?" he shouted.

"Anywhere that's away from you."

"You can't walk home from here."

"Watch me," she yelled over her shoulder. She knew he was right, but she was so upset, so angry she'd made such a fool of herself over a kiss, she didn't care.

He caught up with her a few steps later and grabbed her arm. "Don't be stupid."

"Thanks for the advice, Officer, but I'm afraid it would have been more useful to me an hour ago." She jerked her arm free and turned to walk away again.

He snagged her wrist and pulled her back against him. "Listen to me, you little fool. This is a very nasty part of town." His voice was barely above a whisper as he glanced around. "And there are plenty of unsavory characters here who wouldn't think twice about taking advantage of a sweet-looking thing like you."

She gave him the best head-to-toe once-over she could manage standing so close to him. "Tell me about it."

"Dammit, would you be reasonable," he shouted, no longer making any attempt to keep his voice down. "I've got two dead bodies, no physical evidence to speak of because the damn rain washed it all away, and not a hope in hell of solving these murders unless I get real lucky or someone decides to cooperate and help us out. Now, I'm sorry I wasn't honest with you when I brought you here, but at the time, it seemed like I didn't have much choice."

"But you didn't have to *kiss* me!" she yelled. She spun away, and as she did, her shoulder bag swung out from her body and smacked him hard in the ribs.

She whirled back around, eyes wide as she stared at him. He stared back, one hand covering his ribs.

"Ohmigod," she whispered. "I'm sorry. Are you all right?"

Hoyle dropped his hand. He was fine; the blow had simply caught him off guard. "Don't worry, Becky. I'm—"

"Here, let me help you." She rushed over to him and started rubbing his side. He had the impression she was trying to make it feel better, sort of the way a mother did when her child had a nasty bellyache.

Well, he had an ache, all right, but the discomfort was located well below his belly, and she wasn't alleviating the problem, she was *causing* it.

Funny, but it seemed that almost anytime she touched him, he had the same strong physical reaction. It was getting to be downright humiliating. He grabbed her hand to stop this latest example of her first-aid skills before the embarrassing effect became more obvious.

"Come on, it's time we got out of here." He dragged her to the car, opened the door, and settled her in the passenger seat.

"Where are we going now?" she asked as he got in behind the wheel.

He started the engine, threw the car in gear, and pulled away from the curb. Both hands on the wheel, eyes straight ahead, he turned left at the corner, taking them back up Main Street and away from the seedy part of town.

"You're taking me in, aren't you?" she said. "For assaulting a police officer."

He glanced at her and was immediately enchanted by her teasing smile. "First offense . . ." He shrugged. "I'll let you off with a warning. Anyway, I suppose I had it coming."

She sat back in the seat. "You really mean that?"

"Yes."

"And you're admitting that was an awful thing to do?"

"Downright rotten."

Crossing her arms in front of her, she turned to face him, leaning against the passenger-side door. "Then why'd you do it?"

"I told you—I've got a case to solve."

"So that makes it okay to use people?" she said quietly.

"Yes. No. Hell, I don't know." He shook his head. He'd employed underhanded methods to obtain information more times than he could remember and had never given it a second thought. Until today. "Look, sometimes it's just part of the job, okay?"

And this was one of those times, Becky told herself, feeling pain slice through her as the reality of the situation hit home a second time. She squeezed her eyes shut against the tears that threatened to erupt again, knowing in her heart that the only thing that could be worse than being used would be letting him see how much it hurt.

She took several calming breaths, but as the hurt subsided, her anger returned. How dare he do this to her? How dare he kiss her like he meant it, then take it all back by saying it was all in a day's work? What an uncaring, insensitive—

"Tell me something, Mack. How far do you usually have to go?"

He shot a curious glance her way. "Huh?"

"You know . . . how fast does this technique of yours normally work? Does a kiss or two loosen the tongue and get you the information you want, or do you usually have to go all the way?"

"What are you talking about—?" He looked at

her again. "Wait a minute. Did you think—?" He shook his head. "No way. That had nothing to do with it."

"No? It seems to me like it was all part of the same scheme. Shake up the gullible little school-teacher first, and if that doesn't work, try persuading her to talk with some heavy lip action. And I have to say," she added, giving him a scathing look, "you're very good at your *job*."

He yanked the steering wheel to the right and screeched the car to a halt in front of Crazy Jack's Bar and Grill, then turned off the ignition. It seemed to Becky they both sat motionless for a long time before he laid his arm on the back of the seat, turned, and leaned forward until he was within inches of her face.

"Thanks for the compliment," he said with a tight-lipped smile that told her he knew she hadn't meant it as such. "But before this goes one step further, I think we need to get a couple of things straight here. I admit I kept you in the dark about the true nature of my appointment with Mrs. Denton because I want to solve this case so bad I can taste it. But that isn't why I kissed you."

He reached over and flicked the lever to release her safety belt, then hauled her across the seat and onto his lap, bringing her lips even with his.

"The only reason I kissed you," he added, dropping his voice to a whisper that was as soft as a summer breeze and sexier than an erotic dream, "was because I wanted to."

His mouth came down on hers again, and this time, there was no hesitation. He didn't test her mood with gentle kisses that were meant to persuade. He didn't set a slow, steady pace that would give her a chance to stop him before things went too far.

He kissed her hard, his mouth moving over hers with a skill that was shocking; with a sense of purpose that made it clear that whatever was happening between them, it had nothing to do with his trying to do his job or her wanting to protect a student in trouble. It had to do with a man and a woman and a spark that ignited whenever they got within a few feet of each other. And it didn't seem to matter one bit that they were as different as night and day.

She wrapped her arms around his neck and leaned into him, pressing her breasts against his chest as her fingers tunneled through his hair. She didn't think about the fact that he'd tricked her, or that they were sitting inside a city-owned vehicle in front of a bar on Main Street, smack-dab in the middle of Santa Ana.

Somewhere in the distance, a horn sounded. The door of Crazy Jack's opened and a blast of music burst out, then faded away as the door closed again.

A few seconds later, a couple walked by the car, loudly laughing and joking about something they seemed to think was funny.

Becky ignored everything except the sensations Mack was creating by rubbing his hands up and down her back. It felt heavenly, being held, caressed, kissed until she couldn't think straight.

Her lips parted, and his tongue slipped into her mouth, seeking, exploring, driving her crazy with each slippery caress.

He framed her face with his hands and held her head still while his mouth took several more nibbles. When he slowly raised his head, his reluctant groan told her he hated to end their kiss so soon. Eyes dark with passion, his breathing shallow and labored, he gazed down at her.

"Well, Beck," he finally said as he rubbed his thumb over her bottom lip, "now do you know why I kissed you?"

She stared up at him, unable to do anything but slowly nod her head in response.

"What'll you two have, sugar?" the cocktail waitress asked, directing her question to Mack.

He ordered them a couple of beers, then watched the woman sashay her way through the tables to the bar. With each sway of her generous hips, the ruffled panties she wore beneath her ridiculously short skirt jiggled suggestively.

Interesting work uniform, Becky thought, surprised to find she was envious of the way the waitress filled out that ludicrous outfit in all the right places. Not to mention the fact that she'd fawned all over Mack, acted like they had a special thing going—

Get a grip, Beck. It was just a kiss—one little kiss. The man doesn't belong to you.

But it wasn't just one kiss, she defended silently. It was two. And he'd made it more than clear that he'd considered himself off duty at the time, which meant it had to have been personal.

"Friend of yours?" she asked, hating the way her question came out.

Mack chuckled and shook his head. "Not really. Arriana calls all the cops 'Sugar.' That way, if one of the guys decides to let off a little steam by shooting the place up, she can always tell her boss 'Sugar' did it. That's usually as far as it goes."

Becky took a look around Crazy Jack's, her gaze skimming over the sawdust on the floor, the dart boards covering one wall, and the ancient-looking jukebox that blasted one raucous song after another. It was standing room only, with a good portion of the clientele dressed in police uniforms and the rest much the same as Mack—sport coats with ties loosened, dark slacks. At least half of them had waved to Mack when they'd walked in, so she assumed they were plainclothes detectives like he was. She would have felt safe knowing he'd brought her to a cop hangout—except for that last remark.

"Do these guys really shoot their weapons off in a public place?" she asked.

"Occasionally." He aimed his thumb at the ceiling, and she saw several dents that looked like they could be bullet holes. "The stress gets to you sometimes."

She swallowed. "Is that the way *you* release stress?"

He laughed. "No. I run five miles a day. That burns most of it off."

And explained the rock-hard thighs, she mused. She immediately decided she liked *his* way of coping with stress more, recalling the way his legs had felt strong and firm beneath hers when she'd been sitting on his lap in the car.

Before she got carried away with the memory, the waitress returned with their drinks. Becky reached for hers immediately. She pressed the side of the icy mug to her cheek briefly, half expecting to hear a sizzling sound, then took a sip.

"So the stress is pretty bad, huh?" It was a dumb question, she acknowledged, but it was better than the one about Arriana calling him "Sugar." Besides, maybe if he told her a little bit about his job—and the pressure that came with it—she might understand how he'd come to be such a cynic.

He took a swig of beer. "Let's just say that it feels like you're spitting into the wind every time you walk out the door of the station house."

She wrinkled her nose. "Sounds awful."

"I suppose it does, but that's the way it is. Every year we have too many homicides, too few detectives to work on the cases properly, never enough hours in a day to do all the legwork it takes to solve all of them."

"So many murders, so little time," she said, paraphrasing the popular slogan about men she'd seen on a bumper sticker a few years back.

Mack let out a derisive chuckle. "Yeah, that about sums it up."

"Is that why you use any trick in the book to catch a killer? Because you're overworked?"

"That's part of it, but I have to admit I'm willing to do just about anything to put scumbags—pardon my French—behind bars."

"And sometimes that means playing dirty."

His eyes narrowed. "The bad guys don't play by Robert's Rules of Order, Becky."

"Neither does Mackenzie Hoyle."

Mack raised one brow. *Touché*, he remarked to himself. The uncomfortable feeling he'd experienced the last time she'd nailed him on his anything-goes approach to his job was back. He tried to push it away, tried to justify his actions—at least in his own mind.

Sure he bent the rules, or—more to the point— developed his own particular set of rules, ones he could live with. After all, it was necessary to get the job done, and he'd never once questioned his methods, never once considered them unfair. Until he'd used them on Becky and seen the pain he had caused her.

Still, the real world didn't function the way things did during a role-playing session in the Academy, he reminded himself. If he followed the Patrol Guide he'd memorized so faithfully before earning his badge, his arrest-to-conviction rate would drop in a hurry. And he'd be back on the streets, writing parking tickets.

"Again, I'm sorry I wasn't honest with you," he said, really meaning it. "But if you knew what I'm up against out there every day, maybe you'd under-stand."

She leaned forward across the table. "So tell me. I'd like to understand."

His first impulse was to crack a joke, or simply ignore her request and change the subject. After all, trying to make a fresh-faced schoolteacher compre-hend the daily aggravations a homicide cop faced had to be an exercise in futility.

The intent look on her face kept him from brushing her off, though. She was serious about wanting to hear about his frustrations, and to his surprise, he found himself wanting to tell her.

"Okay, let's say I know for a fact that a guy committed a particular murder," he began, realizing immediately that he was long overdue for a gripe session. And damn lucky to have stumbled onto someone who was willing to listen to his woes. "I have a signed confession, a truckload of physical evidence, *and* a Catholic priest for an eye witness."

"Sounds like an open-and-shut case," she said before taking another sip of beer.

"Sure does, but the fact of the matter is that the odds of me seeing the perpetrator rot behind bars the way he should are pretty slim."

"Oh, come on now."

"Hey, I'm just telling you the way it is. The perp hires himself a hotshot attorney—or some wet-behind-the-ears law school graduate who's looking to make a name for himself—and they look for a way to beat the system."

She reached out and placed her hand on his arm. "I think that's terrible."

He was certain her gesture was meant to underscore her distress at the reality he'd just described. He was equally certain the heat he felt when she touched him had nothing to do with their mutual feelings about the injustices of the legal system.

"I agree," he said, trying to ignore the way her fingers were toying with the hair on his arm. "But it happens all the time."

"I don't get it," she said, shaking her head. "If you know the guy did it and have all that evidence to prove your case, how could he possibly get away with it?"

Mack shrugged. "Sometimes the lawyer plea-bargains the perp down to a lesser charge and he ends up doing a laughable amount of hard time. Or—worst case scenario—the honorable council for the defense finds a loophole in the law and the defendant, who is guilty as sin, walks away scot-free." He gave another shrug. "So I've busted my rear to make sure the charge will stick—and in the end have nothing to show for it."

"That stinks."

She'd spoken the words so softly, he almost didn't hear her, but the look in her eyes—and the gentle touch of her hand—told him every-thing he needed to know. She was on his side, sympathized with his tale of woe. And as much as he hated to admit it, it felt good to know someone understood.

Not just someone, a voice inside his head pointed out. *Becky.*

He shook off the unwelcome distinction, unable to deal with the implications that came with it.

"It's a terrible situation," he said, "but I'm afraid it comes with the territory."

Becky sighed. She knew exactly how he felt. After all, he'd pretty much described the situation she was up against in her own job.

Each year she saw bright, intelligent students—like Arturo—kids with potential who deserved to get an education, to graduate from high school and go on to college or trade schools. But the statistics showing how many actually did just that were pathetic, and she knew that whatever *she* did, no matter how hard *she* tried, there was a better than even chance that all her work would be for nothing.

Still, she persisted. Because she cared. She would never stop hoping that the situation would improve, and that every kid who wanted to make something of himself would get the chance to do so.

The question was, why did *Mack* persist? She wanted to know, needed to know.

"Why do you do it, Mack? If it's all so hopeless, why continue being a cop?"

Deliberately stalling, Mack reached for his beer and took another long gulp. He'd already told Becky far more about himself and his attitude toward his work than he'd ever told anyone outside the police force. If he was smart, he'd give her the it's-my-job routine and let her think that no matter how much he ranted and raved, all he really cared about was collecting his paycheck.

He couldn't do that, though. He'd been less than honest with her once that day already, and he still had a sour taste in his mouth from it. Besides, a cavalier explanation like that was bound to leave her with a rotten impression of him, and as much as he hated to admit it, her opinion of him was beginning to matter.

"I keep at it because every now and then I manage to win one," he said without further hesitation, then held his breath and waited for her reaction.

"You beat the odds," she said, her lips curving into a knowing smile. "That's when you tell yourself it's all worth it, isn't it?"

He nodded, smiling back at her, all the while wondering if she could read his mind. "And you believe it," he said. Without thinking about what he was doing, he reached out and wound a lock of her soft blond hair around his finger, toying with it. "Know why?" he asked.

Her eyes never leaving his, she shook her head.

"Because when all the pieces fall neatly into place and one dirtball finally gets locked behind bars where he belongs, you know the city is just a little bit safer"—he let the silky strand slip through his fingers—"for people like you."

Stunned by his answer, Becky leaned back against the hard oak booth, suddenly realizing she was seeing him, really seeing him, for the first time.

She had to admit his tough-guy act had fooled her. Until now. Now she knew the truth.

The truth was that Mackenzie Hoyle—the cynical, hard-hearted homicide detective who appeared as though he didn't give a damn about anything except catching the bad guys—cared. About people, and about making the world a better place. Just like she did.

Which meant that in spite of their differences, they had that one very important thing in common. As she watched him drain the last of the beer from his mug, she wondered how long it would take the detective to come to the same conclusion.

FIVE

Mack jogged past the Quik Stop convenience store, turned right at the corner, and sailed past the burned-out shell of a movie theater that had been boarded up for two years. Rain fell in a steady drizzle, making it impossible for him to tell if he was sweating profusely or just getting a thorough drenching from the sky.

One more lousy mile, he prodded, dangling the prospect of a quick shower and a pepperoni pizza in front of his nose for incentive. After dinner, he'd stretch out on the couch, turn on a ball game, and tune out everything else. He was so tired, he might even be able to close his eyes that night and not see a beautiful pair of blue eyes surrounded by pale wispy lashes that fluttered seductively when—

Dammit, Hoyle, you're doing it again.

Immediately, he picked up his pace, mercilessly

punishing his body because his mind was torturing him.

Until a few days ago, his daily jog had been a ritual he enjoyed—and depended on. If all went according to his plan, his pavement-pounding routine allowed him to fall into bed physically exhausted and mentally free of the haunting images that too often made it tough for a guy in his line of work to get a decent night's sleep.

If things went according to his plan.

Since meeting a certain woman with hair the color of sunshine, nothing had.

Oh, his solitary jaunts still managed to banish disturbing work images, but that left his mind free to dwell on a subject that did an even better job of keeping him awake half the night—Miss Rebekah de Bieren.

Each breath he drew seemed to fill his nostrils with the fragrance of her perfume, the memory so vivid, it made his head spin. He'd clutch the bedding in frustration, only to find himself automatically comparing the coarseness of the sheets to the baby-fine texture of her hair.

Closing his eyes against the images made the situation even worse. He'd picture his fingers caressing flawless skin, see her lips part when he ran his thumb over them, feel himself grow hard just thinking about kissing her again, touching—

Knock it off, Hoyle. She's not your type anyway.

He gave his head a vicious shake and told himself that even though his body was rejecting the last argument, his brain was still in charge. And it was telling him—loud and clear—that he had no business getting involved with Becky.

She was a dedicated schoolteacher with a heart as big as Alaska. He was a homicide cop with a terminal case of cynicism.

Plain and simple, it was a match made in hell.

Which was exactly where he spent most of his waking hours—in hell, dealing with unreliable informants, reluctant witnesses, and cold-blooded murderers. Not what you'd call a well-rounded life, he willingly acknowledged, but he was reasonably content with the status quo.

When and if he ever found himself wanting to balance things out by adding a personal relationship to the equation, he wouldn't be stupid enough to think it would work with someone like Becky. She was too sweet, too gentle, too vulnerable to handle his job and the kind of life that came with it. In spite of how good it had felt to be on the receiving end of her sympathy and understanding, he knew it would be wrong to allow her to get mixed up with him.

As it was, he regretted exposing her to his world in the first place, when he'd taken her to see the Denton widow and her kids. He'd have to be one lousy bastard to subject her to any more of it. And he hoped to hell he wasn't that far out of control.

He wasn't, he told himself, feeling safe in the knowledge that he couldn't possibly be in too deep after only one kiss.

Two kisses, a voice inside his head amended with ruthless honesty.

The unwanted reminder startled him, causing him to lose his concentration and trip over a gaping hole in the sidewalk. Arms flailing, he stumbled along for several seconds before regaining his stride.

"Cripes, I could have fallen and cracked my fool head open," he muttered with disgust, then shot a couple of imaginative curses over his shoulder at the offending concrete. Rounding the corner onto his street, he slowed to a pace barely above a brisk stroll, thinking he shouldn't be this tuckered out from a run that was no more strenuous than usual.

Halfway down the block, he came to an abrupt halt. He blinked, then rubbed a damp forearm across his eyes to try to clear his vision. He must really be losing it, he decided. This time his imagination had conjured up Becky in the flesh. Standing in the middle of his porch, no less.

He shot a glance to the right and caught sight of her sporty yellow car—parked in *his* driveway—and realized his mind wasn't playing tricks on him after all. She was there, all right.

Hoping to give his pulse a chance to slow to normal, he took his time walking the rest of the way to his house. His stall tactics didn't do much good, though, because his heart was still hammering as he strolled up the walkway to his porch.

She was holding a bright red umbrella over her head, and a pair of red high-top sneakers poked out from beneath a red plastic rain slicker. A red-and-black-plaid picnic basket was perched on the step next to her.

When he stopped in front of her, she tipped her head back until her gaze locked on his. She smiled, and the fatigue that had plagued him for the last twenty minutes vanished.

That was when he realized, with a sinking feeling, that he was far more out of control than he'd thought.

Becky wandered around Mack's living room, too nervous to remain in any one spot for more than a few seconds.

Maybe she shouldn't have come there, she thought. She immediately quelled her doubts by reminding herself that she had information about Arturo that Mack would be eager to hear.

Of course, she could have picked up the telephone and saved herself a trip. Instead, she'd stuffed a picnic basket full of food and traipsed over here to deliver the news in person. As she battled rainy weather and the traffic snarls that inevitably came with it, she tried to convince herself that the impromptu dinner party to celebrate her breakthrough with Arturo was for Mack's benefit.

It was, she told herself once again as she detoured around the coffee table and traced the perimeter of the braided rug in front of the fireplace. After all, the man was way too serious, way too much of the time. He desperately needed to learn how to relax and have a good time every now and then. A rainy-day picnic would make an excellent first assignment, she'd decided on the spur of the moment.

Finally pausing in front of an overstuffed easy chair, she snagged a throw pillow that had been tossed onto the seat cushion. Who was she trying to kid? she wondered, hugging the pillow to her chest. The main reason she was standing in the middle of Mackenzie Hoyle's living room was because she was attracted to him and had wanted to see him again.

For several days now, she hadn't been able to stop thinking about him. Whenever she closed her eyes, she heard his voice; pictured the clear gray color of his eyes and the lock of hair that kept falling down onto his forehead; recalled with remarkable accuracy the way it had felt to have him hold her tight and rub her back as he tried to soothe her when she'd cried.

Most of all, she remembered the way he'd kissed her. Twice.

She shook her head to clear her mind, but the memories remained, forcing her to acknowledge again that something had happened between them the other night, something crazy and exciting and completely unexpected.

At first she'd tried to chalk up her reaction to Mack's kisses as hormones run amok. After all, it had been a long time since she'd had a steady boyfriend. She was bound to have an excess of sexual energy stored up and waiting for an outlet.

But then she'd realized that even though she hadn't had an intimate relationship with a man in quite some time, she did date frequently, and more often than not her dates ended with a kiss or two on her front porch.

Friendly kisses, maybe-we-should-go-out-again-soon kisses, I-had-a-nice-time, how-about-you kisses.

Kisses that hadn't come close to setting off fireworks the way Mack's had.

In the end, she'd wound up admitting her reaction to this particular man had nothing to do with wacky hormones or an overabundance of sexual energy, but she still wasn't any further ahead in understanding what attracted her to him. So she'd decided the only way to solve the mystery was to spend some time with him and get to know him better.

Which meant her picnic would do double duty, she told herself as she tossed the pillow back down on the chair. It bounced once before landing right side up.

Immediately, her gaze was drawn to the names that had been stitched in needlepoint across the face of the pillow, names that made up the Hoyle family tree. She reached down and picked the pillow back up again. Mack's name occupied the lowest branch on the tree, and just above him in neat gold stitches were the names of his father—Joseph P. Hoyle—and mother—Colleen E. Mackenzie.

Pleased with her discovery, she turned toward the center of the room, deciding to explore further.

Mack lived in a small house on a quiet residential street in one of the better neighborhoods in Santa Ana. Each room she sneaked a peek into was neat as a nuns' residence. No dirty dishes cluttering up the kitchen sink and counters, no wet towels littering the floor of what appeared to be the guest bathroom.

A half-finished jigsaw puzzle was spread out over the better part of the dining room table, but the unplaced pieces were organized by color into several groups, with a few straight-sided pieces by themselves.

A place for everything and everything in its place, she concluded, not at all surprised to discover Mack's passion for law and order extended beyond work.

Once she'd pretty much covered the territory she could see without invading his privacy entirely, she wandered back into the living room and paused in front of the picture window. As she looked out over the neatly trimmed front yard, she could hear the steady sound of the shower coming from somewhere down the hall, where the master bedroom must be located.

Without warning, she found herself imagining what it would be like to stand naked with him beneath the hot water, soapsuds sliding down their slippery bodies as their hands slid over each other. . . .

The water shut off abruptly—just in time to cut off her fantasy before it got totally out of control. Several minutes later, she heard the bathroom door open. The crisp, clean scent of soap, combined with the spicy aroma of after-shave, wafted into the living room. She drew in a deep breath, and the pleasant mixture tickled her nostrils.

"So how'd you get my home address, *Detective* de Bieren?"

Mack's voice had come from one of the bedrooms, where she could hear him pulling on a pair of pants. She smiled at the way he gave her credit for tracking him down at home.

"I went to the station house," she said, raising her voice to make sure he could hear her, "and—"

"Charmed the desk sergeant out of classified information? I've been told that's cheating—*teach*."

She laughed. "I didn't use any underhanded tactics, I promise. I simply told him I had important information for you concerning a witness in one of your murder cases, and that it was imperative that I meet with you at once. But you know"—she gave a nervous laugh—"I think he suspects there's something romantic going on between us because he—"

A hand gripped her upper arm, cutting her off midsentence and whipping her around. She fell against Mack and brought her hands up against his bare chest to steady herself.

Swallowing a gasp, she instantly concluded that jogging did more for this man than reduce stress and create rock-hard thighs. It produced a lean, mean muscle machine that was impressive as all get-out— especially when only half clothed.

"What information?" he asked, holding her far enough from him so that she could see his face.

She glanced down, following a trail of dusty brown hair as it bisected his chest and disappeared into the waistband of his jeans. Involuntarily licking her lips, she slowly raised her head until her eyes met his again.

"Uh . . . Arturo came to talk to me this morning," she said, trying to keep her fingers from curling around the soft hairs beneath them. "He heard the news reports about Frank Denton being murdered."

"And he's worried that the same thing could happen to him, right?"

"He didn't come right out and say so, but yes, I think that was why he came to me."

"He should be. What did you tell him?"

"I told him that if he knew anything at all that might help you catch the murderer, he should talk to you."

"What did he—?"

"Mack, *I'm* scared too. What if—?"

"Take it easy, Beck." He brought his hand up and smoothed a wayward strand of hair off her cheek. "Did he agree to talk to me?"

She nodded. "Reluctantly."

Mack set her away from him and started for the bedroom. "Good. I'll get right over to his—"

"Wait." She grabbed his arm. "You can't go to his house. He won't talk to you if he thinks anyone else will find out."

"Then how am I supposed to—?"

"He'll meet with you tomorrow—at my house. He rides his bike over every Saturday to mow my lawn. And he promised me he wouldn't go to work at the liquor store tonight," she quickly added. "He'll stay home—where he's safe—until he can talk to you."

Hands on his hips, Mack began to pace, mumbling to himself and nodding his head. His bare feet made no sound as he traveled from one end of the living room to the other and back. On the third pass, he stopped in front of her, then brought his hands up to cup her face. His mouth came down on hers for a quick, hard kiss. Becky felt a tingling sensation sail from her tummy to her toes.

"Good plan, Detective de Bieren," he said, smiling.

She let out a halfhearted sigh. She was glad Mack had decided the arrangements she'd made were satisfactory. If Arturo really was a key witness in this case, though, she wouldn't be able to relax completely until the murderer was in custody and Arturo was out of danger.

Now she was doubly thankful she'd thought of the picnic. It would provide a distraction from worrying about this whole situation, at least for the night. She pointed to the basket she'd set down near the coffee table.

"Now that we've gotten that out of the way, how about a picnic?" she asked.

Mack followed the direction of her finger and drew his brows together in a questioning frown. "Here?"

"Sure. Why not?" She tipped her head to one side and gave him a challenging stare. "Unless you know of some law that says it's illegal to have an indoor picnic on a rainy day, Officer."

That earned her a grin. "Don't go 'way. I'll be right back," he answered, and headed to the bedroom to finish dressing.

Mack split the last of the bottle of wine Becky had brought between their two glasses, then tossed the empty bottle into the picnic basket.

It had sounded like the craziest idea he'd ever heard of—having a picnic indoors on a rainy day. It had turned out to be the most enjoyable evening he'd spent in a very long time. In fact, he'd managed to make it through the entire meal without thinking about witnesses, physical evidence, possible suspects. Amazing.

But the relaxed mood he was in had little to do with eating fried chicken on a blanket in the middle of his living room floor, he acknowledged. His dinner companion deserved most—if not all—of the credit for the way he was feeling.

Normally, an admission like that would have startled him into throwing all of Becky's picnic paraphernalia in that plaid basket of hers and ushering her out of there in a hurry. That he wasn't doing exactly that should have scared the hell out of him as well.

It didn't, though, and he couldn't say why. All he knew was that he was having a good time, and for the moment, he didn't want to worry about the fact that he was enjoying her company more than he had a right to.

"So you graduated from college, spent a couple of years in the Peace Corps . . . then what?" he asked, eager to discover more about her.

She was sitting across from him, her legs stretched out in front of her, one hand propped behind her. The red-and-white-patterned leggings she wore hugged her ankles, her calves, her thighs, revealing just about everything those baggy parachute pants she'd been wearing the day he'd met her had hidden. Her white sweater, on the other hand, would have been more to his liking if those curvy scallops along the bottom hem had stopped somewhere around her waist instead of about midthigh. The neckline more than made up for the overly long length, though, as it kept slipping down on one side to give him a view of a creamy soft shoulder and a pure white satin bra strap.

"I came back to the United States for a much-needed vacation," she answered, spearing the last slice of peach from the container of fruit salad and bringing it to her lips.

As he watched, her tongue came out to meet the succulent morsel a split second before her mouth closed over the fork. Mack licked his own lips and could have sworn he tasted the peach himself.

Peaches, he realized with a start. That was the fragrance of her perfume, the elusive scent that had been driving him crazy for days. Juicy, vine-ripened, melt-in-your-mouth sweet peaches.

Though he knew he was allowing his mind to wander into dangerous territory, he couldn't help wondering if she smelled like that all over. Without warning, he found himself aching to discover if she dusted her entire body with peach-scented powder after a shower, dabbed the mouth-watering fragrance behind her ears, at the base of her throat, behind the backs of her knees—

He cleared his throat. "And ended up teaching at Benito Juarez?" he asked, half-surprised he was able to remember what they'd been talking about.

She shook her head. "Not right away. I had to take a job as a counselor at a school in Newport Beach for a year before the position at Benito Juarez became available."

"Wait a minute," he said. The angry tone of his voice startled him, until he realized he *was* angry with her. It was one thing for her to take a job in a lousy area if she'd needed the work, but she'd voluntarily put herself in danger every day. "You gave up a position in a nice, safe city like Newport Beach to teach in a school where the kids throw rocks through the windows on a daily basis?"

Becky tipped her head to the side and gave him a serious look. "Sounds crazy, I know. But Juarez offered me a position that combined teaching and counseling, which is more interesting, and, well . . . the truth is, I didn't think they really needed me in Newport."

"And you need to be needed," he commented, more to himself than to her.

He'd already concluded that compassion and a desire to help others was in her blood. Her parents ran a nonprofit organization that provided aid to underprivileged people all over the world, and she'd spent most of her school vacations working side by side with them.

Which meant she wasn't nearly as naive as he'd first assumed. She'd seen more misery and suffering in her travels as a child than most people would in a lifetime of watching CNN.

No, she wasn't naive, he decided, just incurably optimistic. And oh so trusting. Which was one of the things he liked most about her, that she'd managed to maintain a positive outlook on life in spite of the experiences she'd had. Once again, it occurred to him what opposites they were.

"What about you, Mack?" she asked as she

stretched out on the floor and propped her head up with one hand. "What do you need?"

"Well, let's see . . . a good clean bust, a respectable clearance rate on my homicide cases." He shrugged. "A fair-minded judge would be nice. If one can be found."

She frowned at him. "There has to be more on your wish list than work-related stuff. What about your personal needs?"

An alarm sounded in his head, shooting a warning signal from his brain to his toes before he had a chance to blink.

The smart thing to do, he cautioned himself, would be to avoid any discussion of his personal needs—especially the ones he'd been aware of for several days now that concerned her. But he seemed to have developed a certain pattern of behavior specific to the woman lying in front of him, and "smart" was the last word he'd use to describe it.

Without taking his eyes off her, he set his wineglass down. Still seated with his legs stretched out in front of him, he leaned closer. He knew full well that he was opening a door he might not be able to close.

"There is one thing I seem to need a lot lately," he said.

Becky allowed herself a deep breath. "What, Mack? What is it you need?"

"You."

"Me?" Her heart started to pound so hard, she could feel it in her ears. She saw him nod slowly as he traced her lips with the tip of his finger. His gaze followed the progress of his finger like that of a starving man who'd suddenly caught sight of an entire banquet of goodies—and she was dessert.

"For days now I haven't been able to think of much else," he continued, his eyes darkening with desire. "The need to see you, hold you, kiss you again. I can't seem to stop wanting you, no matter how hard I try."

"Why try at all?" she asked, puzzled by his resistance.

"Because I know it's wrong." He leaned closer and kissed one eyelid, then the other, then moved over to treat the rim of her ear to the same delicious attention he'd given her mouth a moment earlier.

She smiled inwardly at the way his actions so thoroughly contradicted his words. "Wrong? For a man to want a woman?"

He lifted his head and gazed down at her. "In this case? " he whispered. "Hell yes. And if you have so much as an ounce of self-preservation in you, you'll pack up that picnic basket of yours and hightail it out of here. Now," he added, letting loose a ragged breath.

"Before the Big Bad Wolf eats Little Red Riding Hood?"

"This isn't a joke, Becky," he said, a melancholy expression on his face. "You should get the hell out of here while you still can."

She reached up and brushed that stubborn lock of brown hair off his forehead. She'd never felt this strong an attraction for any man, and he was crazy if he thought he could scare her away. The magic that was happening between them felt right to her, and she knew that if he gave it a chance, he'd feel it too.

"I'm not going anywhere," she said, her mouth curving into a confident smile.

Mack closed his eyes, then opened them again and took her chin in his hand, forcing her to look straight at him. "Dammit, Beck," he muttered, "you don't have any idea what you'd be getting into if you got involved with me."

"Oh, but I think I have a very good idea," she said, and lifted her chin in a gesture of pure defiance.

Deep down inside, Mack knew nothing could be further from the truth, and if he'd been able to dredge up even a speck of self-control, he would have gathered up her stuff himself and sent her on her way.

But when she closed her eyes and parted her lips,

silently daring him to ignore the invitation she was offering, he knew he couldn't resist her. Lord, help him, he just couldn't.

He leaned closer and slid one arm around her waist, then lowered his head until a scant inch separated their mouths.

"Okay, Becky, have it your way. But don't say I didn't warn us," he said softly, then touched his lips to hers.

What the hell do you think you're doing? the voice inside his head screamed.

Whatever the hell I want to, he answered, ignoring the warning the same way he'd ignored every other one since this little bit of sunshine had walked into his life.

He knew she was all wrong for him. He knew he was all wrong for her. But he wanted her and she wanted him, and at that moment nothing else mattered.

Her mouth was soft, cool, tasting of wine. The kiss, though, was far more intoxicating than the alcohol he'd consumed. He drew her closer. Empty wine goblets clinked together and tumbled over, landing somewhere on the blanket beside them. With his free hand, he swept the glasses out of the way, then pulled Becky onto his lap.

He rolled onto his back, taking her with him, one arm wrapped around her waist while the other hand cradled the back of her head to keep her lips tight against his.

He barely noticed her weight, but he did notice everything else about her body, especially the way it felt against his. The way her soft breasts were crushed against his chest, the way he could span her tiny waist with his hands, the way she seductively swayed from side to side when he raised his hips and pressed his hardness into her.

He teased her mouth with his tongue, licking and sipping and drawing circles over her full bottom lip. She responded with soft mewing sounds, like a hungry kitten begging for more. He plunged into the warm recesses of her mouth and found it still wasn't enough. For either of them.

Holding her tight, he rolled to his side and kept going until she was beneath him. Her hands were in his hair again, kneading his scalp, then gripping handfuls to hold him steady as she lifted her head to attack his mouth.

He almost smiled at her bold moves. She made love the way she seemed to do everything else—with all her heart, holding nothing back, risking it all. And he was selfish to let her. Later, he'd kick himself for taking a gift as precious as her trust. Later, when his brain was functioning once again.

His hand slid beneath the hem of her sweater and up her body to cup one breast. Through the satin covering, he fingered the nipple into a tight bud, then eased the material aside. He brought his head down and let his lips close over the pink tip, drawing it into his mouth the way he'd wanted to days ago, when she'd accidentally fallen against him and set him on fire. Her hands digging into his shoulders, she arched up to him, driving him wild with her need to get closer.

You never should have started this, that cockamamy voice in his head taunted.

He knew there was nothing in the world that could make him back off at this point.

"Mack?" A woman's voice called. "Are you in there?" Three loud knocks on his front door followed.

Nothing in the world, he repeated silently, *except . . .* Even half crazy with desire, he recognized that voice.

Reluctantly, he cracked one eye open and looked down at Becky. Her lips were moist and pink and swollen from his kisses, and the corners of her mouth were turned up in a contented smile.

"Beck?" He caressed her cheek with the back of his hand, aching to test the smoothness of her skin with his lips.

As if he were trying to rouse her from a pleasant dream before she was ready to wake up, she stretched her arms up over her head. The lazy action caused her breasts to press more firmly against his chest. "Hmmmm."

He bit back a moan. "Open your eyes, sunshine."

She wrinkled her face in protest, then opened her lids one speck at a time. "Why?"

"I'm afraid the Maternal Order of Chastity has arrived." As if to prove his point, the pounding on the door increased in volume.

She turned her head in the direction of the noise, then looked back at him, her eyes widening in surprise. "Your *mother's* at the door?"

He nodded once. " 'Fraid so."

SIX

Becky told herself not to panic. They'd only been necking. *Serious* necking, yes, but his mother hadn't actually caught them *doing* it. In fact, she realized with a start, Mack's mother had probably knocked on the door in the nick of time.

She pushed Mack off her, then clumsily scrambled to her feet. Unintentionally, her thigh brushed against the lower region of his body.

He closed his eyes and let out a low moan of pleasure. "Ummm . . . do that again, would you?"

Tugging the hem of her sweater back down to her thighs, she glared at him, horrified that he hadn't already leapt to his feet to get the door. She couldn't believe this was happening.

"Would you please get *up*?" she whispered,

forcing one word out at a time between gritted teeth.

"I can't." He rolled onto his stomach and buried his face in his forearms.

She shot a glance over her shoulder at the door. The pounding noise was definitely getting louder. "You have to."

"For cripes' sake," he said in a muffled voice, "I'm in no condition for a visit from my *mother*."

Becky reached down and rolled him back over, intending to help him to his feet, then stifled a frustrated groan when she discovered he was right. There was no way he could answer the door, looking like he'd bought a pair of jeans that was several sizes too small—in the crotch.

"Come here, I think I can fix the problem." She grabbed his hand, dug her heels into the carpet, and leaned back until she'd pulled him up into a sitting position.

He tugged on her hand and she tumbled into his lap. His grin was wicked. "I'm sure you can, sunshine," he said as he lowered his mouth to hers.

She ducked her head. His lips grazed her neck and sent a shiver down her spine. She pushed her hands against his chest and gave him a suspicious look. "Are you drunk?"

He shook his head. "Uh-uh. I think I'm in love. She gasped, then decided he must be teasing her.

"Stop fooling around," she ordered as she pushed against his chest and managed to break free. "We've got to do something—fast."

"I agree." His grin widened into a smile, then turned to a disappointed scowl as she scooted away and got to her feet.

"Stand up," she said. He took his time complying with her order. "I have a plan."

"Me too," he said, pumping one eyebrow up and down so vigorously, it was impossible for her to miss his meaning.

"We'll go with mine," she answered, wondering how he could be so cavalier about the situation. He *must* have had too much wine. She grabbed his shirt in both hands, pulling up until she had the entire thing untucked.

"Hey, great minds think alike," he said. Still grinning, he undid a button.

She batted his hand away, then tipped her head down so he couldn't see she was trying to hold back laughter. This was a Mack she'd never seen before— obviously tipsy, wickedly suggestive, just having a good time. She liked this side of him, even though he wasn't taking the situation with his mother seriously.

Trying to ignore the way he was running one finger down the side of her neck and across her shoulder, she grabbed hold of his shirttails and gave them a yank until the front of his jeans was completely covered. "There's, that's better."

He looked down, then back up at her, pulling one corner of his mouth into a sassy smirk. "Thank you, Coco Chanel," he said, "but we would have had more fun with my plan."

Ignoring the comment, she put her hands on his shoulders, turned him around, and pushed him toward the door. "Don't keep your mother waiting any longer, Romeo."

Mack shuffled to the door and swung it open with more force than intended. Suddenly realizing he was none too steady on his feet, he grabbed the top of the door for balance.

One hand raised to knock again, his mother stared up at him. "Thank God you're all right," she said, and heaved a huge sigh.

Mack glanced over his shoulder at Becky, thinking he'd have been a lot *more* all right without this interruption. "What brings you out on a rainy night like this?"

"I watched both the five and six o'clock newscasts, but they didn't mention anything about a shoot-out, and—". Colleen broke off, finally noticing Becky standing near the sofa. "Oh, I'm interrupting," she said, and ran a shaky hand over her hair, pushing a few brown wisps away from her face.

"Of course not," he lied as he took her hand

and pulled her in across the threshold. "Come on in. There's someone here I'd like you to meet."

Once the introductions were made, Colleen turned back to Mack. "When you didn't show up for dinner tonight—"

"Dinner?" He gave her a puzzled look, then closed his eyes. "Oh, no," he said, sobering instantly. "This is Friday, isn't it?"

Colleen nodded.

Becky listened to the exchange, noted the strained look on his mother's face, and realized Mack must have been expected at his mother's house for dinner that night.

"Cripes, Mom, I'm sorry. It completely slipped my mind. Why didn't you call?"

"I did. And when I didn't get an answer here, I called the station house to see if you had to work late, but they told me you were off at five. Then I decided to—"

"Oh, for crying out loud. This was my first night off in weeks, so I unplugged the damn phone before I got into the shower." He muttered an expletive under his breath and shook his head. "I'm sorry you—"

"It's okay. These things happen. Don't give it another thought," she said, cutting off his apology while giving him a gentle pat on the cheek.

Becky heard the tremor in Colleen's voice, and

she would swear the cheerful smile Colleen gave her son was forced, especially considering the panicked expression she'd been wearing only minutes before. No matter what she said, Colleen was upset about Mack having missed their dinner together. And Becky knew she was to blame.

Mack folded his arms across his chest, a thoughtful expression on his face. "I'm sorry you had to go to the trouble of coming over here on a rainy night," he said quietly.

His mother dismissed his concern with a wave of her hand. "I had a few things I needed to pick up at the grocery store anyway. Aunt Sissy's at the house with—"

"Aunt Sissy?" Mack interrupted. He stepped forward and, grabbing his mother by the elbow, led her to the couch. Placing his hands on her shoulders, he pushed down until she was seated. "How is she?"

Colleen tipped her head back and gave her son a strange look. "She's fine. What on earth—"

"How about something to drink? You must be thirsty from the trip over here."

Colleen drew her brows together. "Trip? I live a mile away."

"I'll get you some water," he said, ignoring her answer.

Becky watched Mack rush off to the kitchen, baffled by the exchange she'd just witnessed.

"So . . . you live close by?" she asked Colleen, hoping Mack wouldn't be gone too long. She felt incredibly awkward trying to make conversation with his mother, especially considering the scene Colleen had unknowingly interrupted.

Colleen nodded. "On Belmont Avenue. It's the house in the middle of the block—the one with the green shutters on either side of the kitchen window."

"Sounds wonderful," Becky commented. Finding it impossible to stand still, she wandered over to the fireplace and glanced at the framed photos on the mantel. One in particular caught her eye, and she picked it up to get a better look.

Mack was standing with an older man in front of a three-story brick building. Both wore the uniform of the Santa Ana Police Department. The older man had his arm draped over Mack's shoulders and a big smile on his face.

"That picture was taken the day Mack graduated from the Academy," Colleen said. "The man with him is his father, Joseph."

Becky had already guessed as much, and wondered how she'd missed the photograph when she'd been looking around earlier. "The resemblance is remarkable."

"Yes, they're alike in many ways. Joe was—" Colleen stared at the picture in Becky's hands and appeared to be lost in thought for several moments. When her eyes finally met Becky's again, they were filled with an emotion Becky couldn't identify. Sadness? Regret maybe? Before Becky could decide, Colleen blinked a couple of times, drew in a deep breath, and smiled. "He was so proud of his son that day."

Becky ran her fingers along the top of the picture frame. "So . . . Mack's father is a policeman too," she said, more to herself than to Colleen.

"Yes," Colleen answered, "and a darned good one."

Becky had to smile at the vehemence in the older woman's voice. "I guess that explains why he looks so happy in this photograph—his son was following in his footsteps. What father wouldn't be ecstatic?"

"Yes, I suppose that's true," Colleen replied, nodding slowly. "Becky, would you mind answering a question?"

Becky looked up. "No, of course not."

"Mack—he didn't tell you about his father, did he?"

"That they're on the force together? Why, no. He hasn't mentioned it, but then, we haven't really known each other all that long. Do they work together, in the same precinct?"

Colleen looked down at her hands. "No. My husband—"

"Took a bullet in the back when he was caught in the cross fire of a shoot-out between two rival gangs," Mack said as he walked back into the living room. "We lost him six years ago."

Becky nearly choked on a shocked gasp. Glancing down at the picture she was still holding, she wished she'd never noticed the darned thing. She raised her head and looked over at Colleen, not knowing what to say.

All the color had gone out of Colleen's cheeks, and her eyes glistened with tears. She opened her mouth as if to say something to her son, then simply stared at him.

She looked truly horrified, Becky thought, as horrified as she must have been when she'd first heard the awful news about her husband. Becky's heart went out to the older woman. Even after six years, the pain was obviously still fresh.

"I'm really very sorry," Becky whispered. Feeling helpless, she set the picture back on the mantel, then shot a frantic look in Mack's direction, begging him with her eyes to tell her what she should do next. He shook his head, and she understood he was telling her to just let the subject go.

"Here, Mom." He held out the glass of water. "Drink some of this."

Colleen shook her head and slowly got to her feet. "Stop fussing," she told him, squaring her shoulders. "I'm fine."

And she did look fine, Becky noticed, marveling at the way Colleen had pulled herself together so quickly. Her cheeks were pink again, and the sadness in her eyes had been replaced by a look of . . . courage? Yes, Becky decided, Colleen appeared to have just fought—and won—some invisible battle over a painful memory. Becky couldn't help admiring her.

"Mom—"

"I think I should get going. I don't like to leave—" She glanced at Becky, then back at Mack. "I should get home."

"No!" Becky said. She scooped up her blanket and wadded it into a ball. "You stay. I need to be on my way."

"Becky, please don't—"

"I should get home," she said, interrupting Mack. "I have some lesson plans I need to work on, a bunch of test papers that need to be corrected . . . I really have to go." She retrieved her coat and umbrella and rushed to the door.

Mack picked up the picnic basket, then walked to the door and handed it to her. "Will you be all right driving home in this weather?"

"I'll be fine. You stay and have a visit with your mother. I'll see you tomorrow morning . . . about nine?" She gave him her address.

Mack nodded, suddenly realizing that with all

that had happened in the last hour or so, he'd forgotten about the important meeting she'd scheduled for him with Arturo. "I'll be there."

She took the basket from him. Turning to Colleen, she said, "It was a pleasure meeting you." Then she was gone.

Mack stood in the threshold for a couple of minutes, his left forearm braced against the frame and his right hand gripping the doorknob. By the time the sound of her car engine had faded into the distance, his knuckles were white.

"Damn." He added several more expletives beneath his breath, then slammed the door shut.

"She's very special, isn't she?"

He whipped around to see his mother standing near the couch. For a moment he'd forgotten he wasn't alone. "I only met her a few days ago," he said noncommittally.

Colleen arched one eyebrow. "I'm your mother, Mackenzie. Don't try to stonewall me."

He took a deep breath. "Okay, *she's* special, but there's nothing special going on between us," he said, wondering exactly who he was trying to stonewall.

For the first time since she'd walked in the door that night, Colleen laughed. "Keep saying that, son. You just might be able to convince yourself it's true."

She walked to the front door, then turned back to face him. "But I doubt it."

For the second time that night, Mack watched a woman he cared about walk out his front door. And for the second time that night, he waited until the car was out of sight before he slammed the door and let loose a string of curse words.

Becky poked at the marshmallow floating on top of her hot chocolate, then absently licked some of the fluffy confection off her index finger. The stack of papers she was supposed to be correcting sat on the table to the right of her, untouched.

Hoping to come up with a different explanation for Colleen's behavior that night, she replayed the scene between Mack and his mother one more time.

Once again she saw the frantic look on Colleen's face when Mack had answered the door, heard the telltale quiver in her voice when she told him she'd watched the news for word of a shoot-out, pictured the way her hand had trembled when she'd run it over her hair in a self-conscious gesture upon discovering her son wasn't alone. And once again, Becky remembered thinking the anxiety Colleen had displayed over a forgotten dinner engagement had seemed excessive—until she'd learned that Mack's father had been a police officer as well, an officer shot in the line of duty.

Becky came to the same conclusion she'd come to every other time—dinner wasn't the issue. Danger was.

Mack had the type of job that would cause any person who cared about him to worry if he was ever late or didn't call—or failed to show up at all, like that night.

A sick feeling curled in the pit of Becky's stomach. It didn't take any effort for her to imagine what Colleen must have gone through until she'd been able to assure herself that her son was unharmed. Becky had suffered similar scares herself many times, the last one occurring a year earlier, when a half dozen civilian relief workers had been killed during a skirmish between rival factions in the civil-war-torn country her parents had been working in.

She remembered how she'd been glued to the television, frantic to hear the name of the relief agency involved; how she'd sat with sweaty palms and a pounding heart, staring at the telephone, hoping it wouldn't ring with the bad news.

Probably Colleen had experienced all that and more. Becky knew she was to blame for having put her through that kind of terror—the terror of not knowing.

She crossed her arms on the table and let her

head rest on them, wondering if Mack would ever be able to forgive her for causing his mother so much pain.

Strong morning sunlight streamed in through the rose-colored curtains on her living room window, bathing the room in a pale pink glow. Becky shifted in the wing-back chair, crossed her legs, and held in the frustrated sigh that threatened to escape her lips. Judging from Mack's tight-lipped expression, she knew he was thinking Arturo had changed his mind about cooperating with the police. She turned her gaze on Arturo.

His hands were clenched into tight fists, and the expression in his deep brown eyes told her he still wasn't completely convinced he was doing the right thing by talking to a cop.

She sat forward in her chair, letting her forearms rest on her knees. She hadn't intended to get involved in their discussion, but it was clear that Arturo was on the verge of losing his nerve. She had to do something.

"You're very brave to come here today, Arturo," she said.

"Or stupid," Arturo muttered.

Mack opened his mouth to say something, but Becky raised her hand to warn him off.

"I think your coming here today," she said, "means you're tired of seeing people get away with murder in your community."

Arturo's laugh was short and cynical. "Yeah, I suppose you could say that."

"And you're letting everyone know that you've got the guts to take a stand when you believe in something."

His eyes narrowed. "I'm not a chicken, if that's what you mean."

"That's exactly the way I see it. You're angry that there's a man out there killing people, and you're willing to do what you can to see that he's stopped." She paused to let that sink in. "And Detective Hoyle wants to help you." Her gaze met Mack's. "You can trust him," she added, smiling. "He's a good man."

Mack doubted he deserved the kind of faith Becky seemed to have in him, but he was sure there was nothing he could say that would convince her of that. And the strange thing was, he felt good knowing she believed in him. Even though she was foolish to do so.

Reluctantly, he pulled his gaze from her and turned back to Arturo. "Go ahead, son. Tell me what you saw that night."

Arturo began slowly, but with Becky's encouragement, the whole story eventually came out.

Mack made notes as Arturo spoke, interrupting only to ask questions when absolutely necessary, which wasn't often. By the time Arturo was finished, Mack was satisfied that he was finally getting somewhere in this case.

He knew, though, that his expertise in interrogating witnesses wasn't responsible for this lucky break. Becky was. Without her gentle coaxing and reassuring presence, Arturo never would have told him a thing.

Mack closed his notepad and slipped it into his coat pocket. "I'm impressed," he told Arturo. "You even managed to get a thorough description of the car, including the license plate number. Most people would have been too frightened under the circumstances."

Arturo seemed to grow taller with the praise. "I was a little scared," he admitted. "But I knew something bad was going down and I wasn't going to run home to Momma like a baby. I had to do something."

"And I'm glad you did. Now, do you think you could pick out this guy's picture if you saw it in a book?" Mack raised his eyebrows doubtfully. "It was awfully dark that night."

Arturo nodded. "They tested our eyes in school about a month ago. I got twenty-twenty vision. Besides, there was a streetlight hanging right over his car, and I got a real good look at him. I'll know him if I see him."

"Good. I'm counting on you." Mack stood up. "Let's get going. The sooner we nail this guy the better."

Arturo stood too. "You got it."

Becky felt the tension that had been building inside her for the last half hour flow out through every pore. In its place was a feeling of tremendous satisfaction. In the past few minutes, an unlikely bond had formed between a young teenager who had grown up learning that cops couldn't be trusted, and a cop who'd made it clear he trusted no one. Pleased that she'd accomplished something positive, she rose to walk them to the door.

"Wait for me in the car," Mack said to Arturo. "I'll be right out."

Becky waited for Mack to close the door.

"Mack—"

"Beck—"

Mack tipped his head. "Ladies first."

"You were right," she said, sighing. "You suspected he was lying from the start, but when you tried to tell me—"

"Hey, I'm a cop, remember?" Mack cupped her face with one hand. "It's part of my job to be suspicious."

She look down at her feet, then took her time raising her head to look him in the eye. "But I thought you were just being a hard-hearted cynic."

His smile was crooked. "I am a hard-hearted cynic."

"And I'm ridiculously naive. It never occurred to me he wouldn't tell you the truth."

"That's what makes you special," he told her as he ran his thumb down her cheek. Arturo had come to her about the trouble he was in because he could trust her not to assume automatically he'd done something wrong. "I'll let you know how this turns out."

She smiled. "Come by later?"

"This could take a while. If Arturo's successful, we may have to go after the—"

"Mack, don't worry about how long it takes." She raised up onto her toes and planted a kiss on his cheek. "I'll make us some dinner, and you can tell me all about your day when you get here. Okay?"

Mack knew he should tell her not to bother with dinner. She'd only be disappointed when he didn't return in time to eat. If he managed to return that night at all.

"I'll be back," he said. As soon as the words left his mouth he realized he'd just broken another one of his rules—the one that said he shouldn't make promises he might not be able to keep.

As he walked to his car he couldn't help thinking that one of these days he was going to have to pay for breaking so many rules, and the price would be steep.

SEVEN

It was after ten o'clock by the time Mack parked his car in front of Becky's that night. He turned off the engine and shot a glance toward her apartment to make sure lights were still burning. A pale yellow glow shone through the curtains of the living room window, letting him know she was there, waiting for him. Still he sat in the car, putting off the inevitable for a few minutes longer.

All day, while he was with Arturo at the station house, then later, when he was trying to locate the suspect the kid had positively identified, Mack's mind had been preoccupied with one thought—that he was an ignorant fool for letting things get so far out of control with Becky the night before.

His mother's unexpected arrival had been a blessing, he'd decided, her appearance a cruel reminder of the vow he'd made six years ago, a vow he'd come way too close to breaking with Becky.

Becky. He zeroed in on the light that was still shining and thought about what she might be doing, how she'd kept herself busy since he'd left with Arturo. No matter what her day had been like, though, he figured she'd be fuming by now.

Waiting wasn't going to make the job ahead of him any easier, he decided. He got out of the car and made his way up her walk.

She answered the door a second after he knocked. He took one look at her and felt desire spring to life so quickly, he knew he was in for a helluva torturous evening. Maybe even the longest—and worst—night of his life.

She was wearing a pair of white lounging pajamas made of a soft shiny material that molded to her curves and left nothing to his imagination. The long-sleeved top had wide lapels and a pocket over one breast, and the trouser-style bottoms sported wide cuffs that broke over the tops of her bare feet. He knew the design was meant to mimic a pair of men's pajamas, but on her the tailored fashion looked a hundred and ten percent feminine.

He meant to tell her he couldn't stay, that he'd only stopped by to apologize for not making it back in time for dinner. And to let her know that last night had been a big mistake.

Before he could get the words out, she reached for his hand and pulled him inside, closing the door behind him.

"Hi," she said, her generous lips turning up in a smile that warmed his insides and made his legs feel wobbly.

He couldn't help himself. He smiled back. "Sorry I'm so late. I'm sure dinner got black a long—"

"Shhh." She used one finger to silence him, then braced her hands on his shoulders and lifted up to press her lips against his. Her tongue slowly circled the perimeter of his mouth, then went around one more time before slipping past the barrier of his teeth for a deep, erotic kiss that left him reeling.

Every good intention he'd ever had about keeping his distance vanished. All he could think about was how great it felt to be holding her, kissing her, being there with her. After spending a near-sleepless night convincing himself he didn't want her, one kiss had managed to thoroughly make a liar out of him.

He wrapped his arms around her and drew her closer, feeling the heat of her body seep through the layers of his clothes. His hands roamed over her, savoring her gentle curves before slipping beneath her top to caress skin that was smooth as satin and infinitely softer than the silky fabric covering it. His thumbs skirted the sides of her breasts, teasing the edges, tracing her shape before toying with her nipples until they contracted into small hard peaks.

He took her lips in a deep kiss, exploring the secrets of her mouth, the dark, warm recesses. Finally, it dawned on him that his actions were thoroughly contradicting his original intent, and after a long moment, he convinced himself he had no choice but to pull away from her.

"Becky." He gripped her shoulders and straightened his arms, locking his elbows so she couldn't get close enough to further weaken his resolve. At the same time he dragged in gulps of air that he hoped would help him regain his common sense. "We've got to talk."

She smiled as she shook her head. "Not before we eat. I haven't had any food since this morning and I won't be able to think straight until I get something in my stomach."

A low growling in his own stomach reminded Mack he'd skipped lunch as well. He caught the scent of something delicious, then lifted his chin and pointed his nose in the direction of the kitchen.

"What smells so good?" he asked, wondering why he hadn't noticed the mouth-watering aroma the moment he'd walked in the door.

Because you were too busy noticing Becky and

her sexy pj's the voice inside his head chided. As usual, Mack ignored the censure.

"Beef stew. It's been simmering in the slow cooker for hours—should be ready any minute now," Becky told him as she slipped her hand in his and pulled him over to the kitchen table. "Sit."

Taking her teacherlike edict in stride, he shrugged out of his jacket and hung it over the back of a chair. After slipping his gun from its holster and placing it on the table within reach, he eased his body down. He wasn't only hungry, he realized, but doggone tired as well. He also noticed the tight coil of tension that had tied his stomach in a knot for the last several hours had disappeared.

Feeling surprisingly content, he watched Becky ladle generous portions of stew over the steaming white rice she'd placed in the center of two plates. After adding a thick slice of French bread to each serving, she carried the plates over and sat down opposite him. He poured them each a glass of burgundy wine from the decanter she'd placed in the middle of the table.

While they ate, he filled her in on the events that had taken place after Arturo had identified their murder suspect, events that had, in the end, amounted to little more than a series of wild-goose chases.

Along with several of his fellow officers, Mack had spent hours searching for Robert Leslie Bailey—

alias Skinny Bob. After running out of leads as to his possible whereabouts, they had finally been forced to call it quits for the night. Tomorrow they'd start all over, leaning on a number of informants they hadn't yet tapped in hopes they'd turn up information that would help them locate Bailey.

In the meantime, Arturo and his family had been placed in protective custody. Becky seemed relieved to hear that last bit of news, and Mack was glad he'd been able to talk the family into accepting police protection.

Once their plates were empty, Becky refilled his wineglass, then urged him in the direction of the living room, telling him she would join him there after she tucked the dishes away in the dishwasher.

Mack stood in the doorway of the kitchen for several minutes while she scraped bowls and rinsed silverware, growing increasingly unnerved by the warm, peaceful feeling settling over him as he watched her perform the simple domestic chore. He knew he should go over to her, shut off the damn water, and insist they talk right now. He'd already hung around longer than he'd intended, far longer than was wise. But she'd made it so easy to stay. And now it was going to be twice as hard to leave.

He found himself wishing the evening had started out the way he'd expected—with her opening her front door, throwing a stone-cold, burned-to-a-crisp dinner in his face, and telling him to take a hike. If it had, it would have been over between them an hour ago. Without the tearful scene that was bound to come when he told her they should stop seeing each other. Without her accusing him of showing an interest in her solely because she was his only hope of getting Arturo to cooperate. Without him having to give away family secrets in a last-ditch effort to convince her it was for her own good that she have nothing to do with him.

Just a quick and easy conclusion to a relationship he never should have allowed to progress beyond one kiss in the first place.

He opened his mouth, determined to get this over with. When she looked over her shoulder to find him still standing there, though, she made a shooing motion with her hand, then turned back to her task, dismissing him again. Taking a realistic look at the situation, he concluded they wouldn't be talking about anything until she was good and ready.

Reluctantly, he walked into the living room and set his wineglass on the coffee table. After taking off his shoes, he stretched out on the couch. He was grateful to have a few minutes to himself after all, he realized as he dangled his feet over one end of the bulbous sofa. Locking his fingers together behind his head, he closed his eyes, intending to take advantage of this time alone to gather his thoughts for the conversation he was dreading. He fell asleep immediately.

Becky spread the wet dish towel over the handle of the oven door to dry, then flicked the light switch off in the kitchen. Picking up her wineglass, she carried it into the living room to where Mack lay on the couch.

She looked down at him. His eyes were closed, and the steady rise and fall of his chest told her he was sleeping. The worry lines that had seemed permanently etched into his face had smoothed out, making him look years younger, and almost care-free.

It appeared as though his unsolved homicide case—along with anything else he might have had on his mind when he'd walked through her door an hour ago—was no longer plaguing him. For now, she thought, and wondered how often he found the opportunity to stretch out on a couch, close his eyes, and forget his worries.

Not often enough, she realized. And he must have been feeling pretty comfortable in her home to be able to relax enough to drop off to sleep so quickly.

She was good for him, she decided. Maybe he

hadn't figured it out yet, but he needed her. He needed a place—a person—to come to that was far removed from the stress and frustrations he faced as a homicide detective. Someone who cared, someone who could help him forget about the ugliness all around him. If only for a few moments. Moments like last night.

Remembering, she smiled down at him, and wondered what he would say if she told him she suspected he'd smiled more last night than he had in the last year. She wondered what he would do if she told him he'd been the picture of contentment all stretched out on her blanket in the middle of his living room floor. She wondered how he would respond if she told him she wished they hadn't been interrupted by his mother.

As Colleen Hoyle's image came to mind, a deep sadness replaced Becky's pleasant memories. What a shame that something that had been so good for Mack had caused his mother so much pain.

She would have to find a way to make Mack understand how sorry she was for the way things had turned out. For all of them.

But that would have to wait, she decided as she walked over to the chair next to the fireplace and sat down. She was determined to let him rest as long as nature intended. After setting her glass on the table next to her and tucking her feet up under her, she picked up the novel she'd been reading earlier. She opened the book and read only a few pages before dozing off.

When Mack awoke, he was disoriented. It had been ages since he'd felt relaxed enough to drop off to sleep with so little effort. His eyes still heavy with sleep, he warily searched the room for some clue as to where he was.

Peering past the end of his feet, he took in the antique brass lamp on the scarred oak end table, the deep rose curtains draped in an old-fashioned style over the living room window, the oval-shaped burlwood picture frame on the wall that held a photograph of someone's great-great-grandmother.

The couch he was lying on was one of those overstuffed things from the forties, and one glance at the frayed edges along the arms and the worn spots on the cushions told him it wasn't a reproduction. It was the real thing.

He knew he wasn't in his own house, and the furnishings seemed vaguely familiar, so he figured he'd been here before. Still groggy, he tracked his gaze to the right until it came to rest on the figure curled up in the wing-back chair in the corner by the hearth.

Becky.

Now he remembered. He'd come to her house expecting to be greeted with anger, disgust, frustration, or any combination of the three.

Instead, he'd walked into heaven—a home smelling like the kitchen of a gourmet chef, a dinner that had no trouble living up to such a promise, a warm woman with a heart-stopping smile and a pair of lips so full and tempting, they could bring a man to his knees.

And, he remembered with a start, he was supposed to wake up this angel and tell her they shouldn't see each other anymore.

What possible reason could he have for wanting to do such a thing?

He gave himself a mental sock on the chin and reminded himself of one very good reason—a woman as good as Becky deserved better than the sort of life she would have if she got involved with him.

Slowly, he rose from the couch, walked over to her chair, and stooped down in front of her. For several minutes, he stared at her, telling himself he needed a moment or two to shake the sleep-induced cobwebs from his brain, trying to convince himself that his procrastination had nothing to do with the intimate feeling that swept over him as he watched her sleep.

Finally, he placed his hand on her shoulder and gave her a gentle shake.

"Beck? Sweetheart, wake up," he said, startled by the husky tone of his voice.

She blinked several times, eyelashes as soft as feathers fluttering against her cheeks until she opened her eyes. Her lips curved into a lazy smile as she raised her arms above her head. The white satin covering her breasts pulled tight, caressing her nipples so that they contracted into hard nubs.

Mack stifled a groan and reminded himself he had an important job to do.

For Becky's sake.

"We have to talk," he said.

She frowned up at him. "I want to go to bed."

"Later."

Later? Now why the hell had he told her that? He should have said *no*, absolutely not, and the reason he didn't nagged at him.

"Why not right this minute?" she asked, puckering her lips into a pout. A soft, tempting, kissable pout.

He closed his eyes and wondered if this could get any harder. If *he* could get any harder.

"I came back here tonight," he said, drawing his words out to give him time to get control over his traitorous body, "because I think it's important that we talk—and that's exactly what we're going to do."

She scrunched her face up and held that pose for a moment. Gradually she relaxed her features, sat up straight, and lifted her chin. She nodded her head once, signaling her consent.

Mack rose and went back over to the couch, slouching down until he was comfortable, happy to have put some distance between them so he could think straight.

To his dismay, Becky followed him, settling her luscious backside down so close to him, their bodies contacted from hips to knees. Then she turned sideways and settled her legs across his lap. To make matters worse, she rested her hands on his shoulder and inched closer, until her breast pressed against his bicep.

"Okay, where do you want to start?" she asked as she toyed with the collar of his shirt.

He sucked in a breath and said a short silent prayer. He was going to need a bit of outside help to get through this.

"With my mother," he said, "and why she was so upset when I forgot about our dinner date."

"I know why," she said, looking down at her hand as she drew a design on his thigh with her fingertip.

He sat up straight. "You do?"

"Yes." She met his gaze. "Because you have a dangerous job and she was worried about you."

Direct and to the point, he thought. Dangerous job equals anxiety for those who care about you. He wished it were that simple.

It wasn't, though. Her words didn't come close to describing the agony his mother had gone through the previous night. Although he would have liked to tell Becky she was right and leave it at that, he knew he couldn't. He had to fill in the missing details for her—without sugarcoating, without using generic language that could be applied to any one of a number of dangerous occupations. He sat up as tall as possible and turned to face her. She tucked her legs beneath her and gave him her full attention.

He looked straight into her eyes. "You're right, she was worried. She thought I was lying facedown in a slime-filled gutter somewhere with a bullet hole in my back."

"Oh, no." Becky's eyes widened, and he could see by the look on her face that she was appalled by the picture he'd painted.

And he'd only told her half of the story.

By the time he was finished, he hoped she'd be able to feel the horror of the situation deep down inside—the way his mother had. Then maybe she'd understand why it would be foolish for her to get involved with a cop.

"And the reason she thought that might have happened to me," he went on in a flat tone that denied the emotional cauldron that was churning his insides into a nasty mess, "was because six years ago, that was the way they found my father."

She covered her mouth with her hand, trying to stifle a gasp, and he knew he'd succeeded in thoroughly shocking her—exactly the way he'd intended.

Still, he felt a stab of mind-numbing pain low in his belly when a pool of tears welled up in her eyes and threatened to spill over.

He sucked in a ragged breath and fought the urge to take her into his arms and comfort her. Somehow, he resisted the equally strong urge to tell her the chances of that actually happening to *him* were slim, not even worth mentioning. He was too careful, too well trained, too good a cop. Because he knew he would be lying if he told her that.

After all, his father had been careful, his father had been well trained, his father had been a hell of a cop.

But it had happened to him.

And now his mother lived with the tragic results every damn day of her life.

Okay, there was maybe one chance in a million of history repeating itself in the exact same manner. Decent odds in almost anyone's book, odds he'd determined he could live with.

The problem was, his mother was forced to live with them as well, whether she wanted to or not. As far as he was concerned, one woman living with that kind of fear in her heart was more than enough.

He wouldn't put another in such an awful position. Becky needed to understand that. Understand it and, more importantly, believe it. Which was why he'd been brutally honest with her.

Without saying a word to him, Becky stood up and walked over to stand in front of the window. Brushing the curtain back, she stared outside for several minutes, looking out into the coal-black night. Finally she turned to face him. Her complexion was unnaturally pale, and her eyes, no longer filled with tears, held an emotionless stare that frightened him.

"She must have been out of her mind with worry," she said in a voice barely above a whisper.

"She's been out of her mind with worry since—"

"And it's all my fault."

"What?" Mack sprang up from the couch and rushed to her side. "That's ridiculous. You had nothing—"

"It's my fault she was upset," she repeated, staring down at her hands. "I never should have come to your hou—"

"No!" His resolve not to comfort her forgotten, he wrapped his arms around her and pulled her into his embrace, crushing her against him, utterly horrified by the way she'd misinterpreted him. He'd been blunt about what his mother had been thinking because he'd wanted Becky to realize she could find herself in that same position someday if she wasn't careful. But he never—ever—intended for her to assume responsibility for last night's fiasco. "It wasn't your fault, Becky."

"Of course it was."

He gripped her shoulders and held her away from him so he could see her face, more determined than ever to make her understand. "Listen to me—you had nothing to do with upsetting my mother."

"But this never would have happened if I hadn't come up with the idea of that silly picnic," she said, sniffling.

"Hey, be careful what you say," he warned, allowing a half smile to curve his mouth and let her know he wasn't angry, not with her, anyway. He was angry with himself for botching this so badly. "That was the nicest picnic I've ever had in my living room . . . on a rainy day . . . in March."

She drew her bottom lip into her mouth and held it there for a few seconds. "I'm so sorry," she said, as if she hadn't heard a word he'd said. "I just thought if I—" She drew in a ragged breath, then sighed. "Oh, I've made such a mess of things, it doesn't matter what I thought."

"Everything about you matters to me," he replied, realizing that despite the number of times he'd told himself he shouldn't care, he did. Placing his finger under her chin, he eased her head up until she was forced to meet his gaze. "Tell me what you were going to say."

She shook her head. "It'll sound silly."

His smile deepened at the way she was making him coax it out of her. "Tell me anyway."

She hesitated another second. "Well . . . I know you have a very serious job and there isn't much to laugh about when you spend all day trying to catch murderers. I wanted to show you how good it feels to forget your work for a little while and have a good time. That's why I came up with the idea for the picnic—because I thought it would be fun." She lowered her head, hiding her face against his shirt. "I just wanted to make you smile," she added, sounding truly miserable.

For a moment, Mack didn't know what to say. He tried to recall a time in his adult life when someone had done something for him that was as sweet and innocent as planning a picnic just to make him smile. He couldn't. He'd never allowed anyone to get close enough to him to care so much about what might make him happy.

He wondered how Becky had managed to breach his defenses, then figured it hardly mattered at this point. The truth was she had. Like a master criminal, she'd slipped past every roadblock he'd put in her way, and if the pathetically sad tone of her voice was any indication, she'd already begun to pay the price.

"Beck, look at me," he said, feeling a sudden need to make her smile.

"What?" she mumbled into his shirt.

"I had a rough day yesterday—"

"Yeah, and I made it worse!"

"No." Again, he urged her head up so that she was looking at him. "In fact," he continued quietly, "you made my day a whole lot better. I felt lousy when I got home last night, and I went out jogging to try to forget some of the stuff that was bugging me. But it wasn't until I saw you sitting on my porch that my problems seemed to disappear. Like magic," he added with a snap of his fingers.

She lifted her chin an inch higher. "I don't believe you."

"You don't?"

She shook her head, then dipped her head down and hid her face from him again.

Her response to his confession took him completely by surprise, especially when he realized with an unsettling feeling that he wasn't exaggerating.

She had the strangest ability to make him forget not only his problems, but everything else too. Like the tried-and-true reasons he'd had for steering clear of her in the first place.

Absently, he rubbed her shoulders, her back, searching for something he could say that would convince her he was telling the truth—because no matter how much he wanted to deny it, it had suddenly become very important to him that she believe him.

"Hey, I'm an officer of the law. Doesn't that count for something?" he asked, grasping at straws.

"Sure," she said, shrugging. "But it doesn't mean you're telling the truth."

"What makes you think I'm not?"

She muttered something he couldn't quite make out.

"Say that again."

She raised her head. Her deep blue eyes sparkled with defiance as she locked her gaze with his. "Everyone lies," she said in a strong clear voice.

Hoyle, you deserved that, he told himself. He had no trouble recalling when and why he'd said that on the day they'd met. He'd told her in a matter-of-fact sort of way that no one—absolutely no one—could be trusted to tell the truth.

He now realized how incredibly smug he must have sounded when he'd recited that first rule in homicide investigations to her as if she were a wet-behind-the-ears recruit.

He also knew, for the first time, what it felt like to be telling the truth and not be believed. It felt god-awful lousy. He grasped her shoulders and pushed her just far enough away from him so that he could look at her.

"Okay, you got me," he conceded. "I admit it. Not everyone lies."

She angled her head to one side and smiled. "I knew that. I was just taking an opportunity to make a point."

Mack let loose a burst of laughter, taken off guard—and, yes, impressed—by the clever way she'd thrown his own words back at him and proved her case at the same time.

Once he had himself back under control, he schooled his features into a serious expression and looked down at her, determined to do whatever it took to convince her she wasn't to blame for what had happened the previous night.

"Then you believe me when I tell you I was so preoccupied with the homicide cases I've been working on that I'd forgotten all about my dinner with my mother long before you ever showed up?"

She looked into his eyes, and he could tell she was still debating. "Well . . . I suppose maybe . . ."

He gave her a little shake. "What happened last night is not your fault," he repeated, suddenly filled with anxiety. He wanted, no needed, her to understand exactly who was to blame. "It's my fault she was upset. Only *mine*."

Becky couldn't help but hear the wealth of emotion in his voice. The intense combination of pain and despair told her that, for some reason, it was vital to him that she believe *he* was to blame for putting his mother through hell. Whether he realized it or not, the anguish she saw on his face told her that the responsibility he carried on his shoulders weighed heavily.

She should have felt relieved to know the part she'd played in last night's fiasco had been minor at the most. But she didn't. Because now she knew Mack's mother had not been the only one hurt when Mack missed their dinner together. Mack had suffered as well.

She reached up and placed her hand on his cheek. "I never realized."

He leaned into her caress. "What?" he asked as he pressed his lips to her palm.

When his mouth moved to nuzzle the sensitive skin on the inside of her wrist, she wondered if he might be trying to distract her from their serious conversation. She refused to let him, because she sensed it was very important.

"I never realized the terrible position you're in," she said. "Forgetting a dinner engagement is usually a pretty minor slipup, but when you have a job like yours it becomes a different matter altogether. That must be awful for you."

He raised his head and stared down at her. "Me?"

"Yes, knowing that one little error could cause

someone you love to feel such heartache and fear—
that's a terrible thing to have on your conscience all
the time."

Mack was speechless. Without him saying a word
to her, she'd known how he felt. Once again, he
wondered if she had the ability to read his mind.

But paranormal powers had nothing to do with
it, he realized. He should have known all along she
would understand—and sympathize with—his pre-
dicament. After all, Becky—the lady with the heart
as big as Alaska—would always manage to find compassion for anyone who needed it.

Not that *he* needed it, of course. Or deserved
it. But he doubted he'd ever be able to convince
her that her concern was misplaced. And now that
he knew she understood, he couldn't help wanting
to talk about the burden he'd lived with since he'd
pinned on his badge.

"I remember the day I came home and told her
I'd passed the entrance exam and was accepted to
the Academy. It must have been the worst day of
her life." He closed his eyes. "Lord, the look on her
face. I'll never forget it."

Becky caressed his cheek, smoothed the worry
lines around his mouth, his eyes. "Don't you think
she might have been just a little bit proud that day
as well?"

He let out a bark of laughter. "Hardly. Now she

had two men in the family who were in danger of getting killed every time they walked out the door."

Instead of backing away with revulsion at his last statement, Becky moved in closer, wrapping her arms around his neck.

"Yes, she did," she said. "Two men who cared enough about the citizens of this community to go out and risk everything—because they think they can make a difference."

Mack shook his head, wondering at her ability to see good where it couldn't possibly exist. Or could it? Was she an impossibly naive fool—or a one-in-a-million treasure?

"Okay, we're convinced we can make a difference," he conceded, "but you tell me this. Why should *she* have to suffer too? Why should she have to pace the floor worrying about something happening to us? Why should she have to eat nine out of ten meals alone because we don't make it home in time for dinner? Why should she risk getting her heart broken by a couple of clowns who've got some crazy notion that they can clean up the streets, beat the odds, and make it home in one piece? Why should she?"

"Because she loves you," Becky said without a moment's hesitation. "And when you love somebody, you take the good with the bad. The happy times and the sad times." Her eyes filled with compassion, she ran one finger gently over his lips. "It's a package deal, Mack. I think she's known that all along, and from what I saw of her, she's strong enough to handle it."

Strong enough to handle it. Mack thought back to the time his father had been wounded in a shoot-out during the robbery of a convenience store. Mack had been twelve years old, and to this day he clearly remembered how calm his mother had been when his father had related the story. He'd laughed and bragged about how the creep who'd tried to kill him had been such a lousy shot, he'd only winged him. His mother had listened quietly, smiling in all the appropriate places, seeming to enjoy Joseph's amusing tale.

That same night, Mack had had a bad dream and gotten out of bed in the middle of the night. He'd wandered out into the living room and found his mother sitting in the dark. Alone. Crying. She'd been clutching the bloody uniform his father had worn to work that morning, the shirt with the small tear in the left sleeve.

She'd put on such a brave front for his father and him—had been doing so ever since. And she'd never once complained.

"You're right," he said to Becky. "She is a very strong woman. But it hurts so damn much to know what she goes through every day of her life because of us."

Becky looked at him long and hard for a full minute, the tender expression on her face gradually fading to one of thoughtful concern. "You know, it's kind of strange," she said in a dreamy, faraway tone of voice, "but until I met you, I always figured the hard part was waiting and not knowing. I never realized it was hard on them, as well," she said, looking away.

Confused by the abrupt change in the conversation, he followed the direction of her gaze to a picture of a man and woman that was sitting on the oak end table. "Your parents?" he asked, realizing she must have been referring to them.

She nodded. "They're always in some godforsaken country where there's a war going on. For as long as I can remember, I've known they could contract some fatal disease or starve to death because the food supplies don't reach them in time—or be killed by a bomb that's been dropped on a hospital by those cruds who don't give a damn about how many innocent people die for their cause."

He drew her closer. "And even though you know it won't make a bit of difference to the outcome in any of those situations, you worry."

She rested against him, her cheek skimming his

chest as she nodded slowly. "Every day. But you've made me understand that *they* live with the knowledge that they're causing that worry. Though I know they could never let that stop them from doing the job they think is important, it still hurts them. Just like it hurts you."

Mack hugged her to him, one hand smoothing over her back as the other caressed her hair, letting the soft blond strands sift through his fingers repeatedly.

He knew she'd just provided him with the best reason in the world for walking out her door and never seeing her again. She already had two people in her life who caused her more than enough grief. It was a sure bet she didn't need to add him to her list.

He was about to tell her that when she raised her head, inched up onto her toes, and pressed her lips against his.

Soft and warm, her mouth moved over his. Brushing first in one direction, then the other, it created a delicious friction that sent heat spiraling southward to an area of his body that didn't need to get any hotter.

Somehow he summoned the strength to break the kiss and take a long step away from her. He had to draw in several huge gulps of air before he could speak.

"Becky, we can't do this."

She tipped her head to one side and regarded him intently. "Why not?"

"I told you before—it's wrong." For so many reasons.

"Then why does it feel so right?" she challenged.

"Because . . ." He clenched his hands into tight fists. Hard as he tried, he couldn't think of a single answer to her question. "Hell, I don't know," he admitted, letting loose a frustrated breath. "What difference does it make anyway? The fact of the matter is—"

"That I want you and you want me. You said so yourself last night," she reminded him, stepping closer. "Or maybe your feelings have changed in the past twenty-four hours." She tipped her head way back and gazed up at him. "Have they, Mack?"

He closed his eyes and muttered a curse. When he opened them again, the first thing he saw was a pair of deep blue eyes glazed with desire. Briefly, he wondered if there was any possible way he could stop this before it was too late.

"What if I said yes, Beck?" he asked quietly, taking a shot in the dark. "What if I told you I no longer want you?"

A series of emotions—surprise, anxiety, uncertainty—flashed across her face in the blink of an eye, then vanished. They left in their wake a look of pure determination that told him he'd missed his target by a mile.

She took another step closer, until there was less than an inch separating them, and eased her hands up his arms to grip his biceps. With a boldness he'd seen only a hint of before, she pressed her body right up against his and slowly swayed from side to side, grazing over the hardening ridge in the front of his jeans in a sexy teasing motion that turned his blood to molten fire and let him know in no uncertain terms he was a goner.

"If you told me you didn't want me," she whispered, grinning like the Cheshire cat, "I'd call you a liar."

EIGHT

Mack groaned and in one smooth move, bent down, wrapped his arms around the backs of Becky's knees, and straightened, heaving her over his right shoulder.

"Which way to your bedroom?" he asked, no longer wanting to fight the desire that had been building inside of him for days.

"Last door on your left, Tarzan," Becky answered with a wicked chuckle, sliding her hands down his back and into the pockets of his jeans. As he carried her down the hallway, she curled her fingers inward and kneaded his rear end.

He gave her a playful slap on the portion of her anatomy that was closest to his face.

"Behave," he ordered in his sternest voice, then

tenderly slid his hand over white satin as he massaged her backside to take the sting out. When the tips of his fingers traveled dangerously close to the incredibly warm spot between her legs, her haughty laughter turned into a distinctively feminine moan of pleasure.

At the end of the hall, he bent his knees slightly to clear the low archway and maneuvered his way through the door and into the center of her bedroom. Leaning forward, he let her go, tumbling her into the middle of the big brass bed.

She landed in a fluffy heap, momentarily sinking into the thick floral comforter, then floated back to the surface and rolled onto her side. With feline grace, she slowly stretched out across the bed, then propped her head up with one hand and smiled at him through pale, feathery lashes.

"I take it this means you still want me," she said.

"Oh, I want you, all right." He grabbed hold of his shirt with both hands and yanked the tails free from his jeans. "I think more than I've ever wanted anything in my entire life."

"More than you want to solve the Denton murder?"

Remembering he'd told her he wanted to solve that case so bad, he could taste it, he nodded. A triumphant gleam glittered in her eyes. He watched that gleam turn to a smoky blue haze filled with desire when he reached for the first button on his shirt and slipped it free.

"More than you want a promotion to . . . say . . . captain?"

He laughed, wondering how she knew that particular ambition of his without him ever having mentioned it. "Yes," he admitted with a chuckle, "even more than that." He finished unbuttoning his shirt and shrugged out of it, letting it fall to the floor next to the bed. "More than anything," he added in a hoarse whisper that was suddenly serious.

Slowly, she got up onto her knees and came over to the edge of the bed.

"Good. Because I want you pretty bad myself, and before this night is over, I hope we both get exactly what we want."

"You can count on it," he promised her, burying his hands in her hair as he cupped the back of her head.

She placed her hands on his legs and tipped her head back to meet his eyes, watching for a reaction to the excursion her fingers had already begun.

She took her time making her way up his jeans, caressing his thighs, coming to within an inch of his groin before taking a frustrating detour back down in the direction of his knees. His muscles tensed beneath her fingertips, and she responded with a knowing smile that reached all the way to her eyes. After an excruciatingly long time, she moved on, continuing her lazy journey with a lack of haste that was driving him crazy.

What's your hurry? We've got all the time in the world, the sly look she gave him seemed to say.

He wrapped his hands around her slender throat, caressing the sensitive skin behind her ears, shocked at how she demonstrated so masterfully that he had less than a tenth of the patience he'd thought he possessed.

Somewhere in the back of his mind he remembered thinking Becky was too pure, too sweet, too innocent for the likes of him. He still thought so, but the pure, sweet misery she was putting him through at that moment was anything but innocent.

And he loved it, he admitted as she leaned forward and placed a wet, openmouthed kiss in the center of his stomach. He clenched his teeth to keep from crying out, then clutched fistfuls of her hair as she left a trail of tiny kisses all the way up his torso.

After a lifetime or two of wandering over his naked chest, her tongue sought out one flat nipple, circling around it several times before she drew the hard nub deep into her mouth. Unexpectedly, she suckled him, and he felt like he'd pitched headfirst out of an airplane—without a chute to break his fall.

Slowly she pulled her head away and gazed up at him. Her eyes were wide with wonder, her chest heaving as she took in huge gulps of air, and he knew she was just as surprised, just as aroused by her erotic behavior as he was.

"Lady, you're playing with fire," he told her through teeth still clenched tightly together.

"Oh, yeah?" Her smile was about as naughty as they come. "I kind of thought I was inventing it," she said, adding a wickedly throaty laugh.

As if to prove her point, she used her thumbs to trace an imaginary line on either side of his arousal, skimming over him so lightly, he would have thought he'd imagined her touch—if he hadn't seen that teasing, promise-filled action with his own eyes. If it hadn't felt like she'd ignited a whole series of incendiary blazes deep down inside of him.

He knew he couldn't take much more of this seductive suffering, that his legs wouldn't be able to hold him up much longer.

Becky wasn't done torturing him yet, though. Her fingers were at his waist now, lingering near his belt buckle, then trailing across the top of his jeans, following the line where rough denim left off and bare skin began.

Before he knew what was happening, she slipped one hand beneath the waistband of his jeans and briefs, dipping low, stroking her knuckles against the sensitive skin of his belly as her fingertips tangled with the coarse hair framing his manhood.

His control finally snapped. He reached down and yanked her to her feet.

She fell against him, gasping for air.

He crushed his mouth against hers in a rough kiss, thrusting his tongue past her lips, past her teeth, deep into her warm darkness.

He felt as if he were trying to brand her, claim her as his—and only his—from this moment forward.

But that was impossible, wasn't it? He would never do anything so cruel to someone as sweet and kind and generous as Becky, would he?

Before he could calm the uncertainties swimming around inside his head, he felt her hands at his waist again, this time fumbling with his belt.

"Help me," she said, when she couldn't get the buckle undone.

I wish I could, he responded silently, knowing he was too far gone to do the right thing. Even if he'd wanted to.

His hands trembled worse than hers as he undid his belt buckle, then the brass fastener on his jeans. With agonizing slowness, he eased the metal zipper down over his swollen flesh.

When he brought his hands back up to his waist to finish undressing himself, she nudged them aside and slid her own hands inside his underwear once again. Freeing him, she wrapped her fingers around him, caressing him with a gentleness that made him ache for more.

Somehow he managed to get his shoes off, then his jeans the rest of the way down his legs and kicked to the side, but it wasn't easy. All the while he was trying to rid himself of his clothes, she was holding him, touching him, kissing him, driving him so far out of his mind, he didn't really know what he was doing.

He only knew he'd never before experienced anything like this. Ever. This was the sort of uninhibited, mind-blowing, all-rules-out-the-window lovemaking that came along once in a lifetime.

And only if you were very, *very* lucky.

She was seated at the edge of the bed now, her legs spread wide so he could stand between them, her hands braced on either side of herself so that she was touching him only with her mouth, her tongue, her teeth. She kissed him, licked him, nibbled the entire rigid length of him, all the while making soft mewing sounds deep in her throat.

When she flicked her tongue around him and finally took him deep into her mouth, he lost control again. He couldn't stand the sweet torture a second longer.

He was buck naked, ready to explode. She still had on every bit of those silky white pajamas.

And, he realized, he hadn't really even touched her yet.

Gently, he put his hands on either side of her head and pushed her away from him. She relinquished his aroused flesh reluctantly. He closed his eyes, savoring the feel of her mouth, the way her teeth scraped against him as she surrendered him one rock-hard inch at a time.

On a groan, he lifted her to her feet, her satin-covered body rubbing against his.

"Time to pay the piper," he said. His voice sounded raspy, as if it took all his effort to get the words out. But then, it had.

"For what?" she whispered. Without waiting for him to answer her, she closed her eyes and gave him a dreamy, self-satisfied smile that told him she knew damn well she'd driven him to the edge.

"For making me want you so bad, I hurt," he told her.

She opened her eyes and looked down. "Hmmmm. I can see I've run up a huge debt." She tilted her head up and gave him a challenging stare. "Do you take credit cards?"

He shook his head.

The corners of her mouth curved into a naughty half smile as she ran her tongue over her teeth. "Good."

Her lips were rosy pink, with a glistening shine that reminded him of the incredible torture she'd been putting him through for who knows how long.

He was way far behind, and his first order of business, he decided instantly, was to catch up. And do a little torturing of his own.

Allowing himself an indecent grin of his own, he wondered if she had any idea what she was in for—what they were both in for—now that he was the one in control. He hoped not, because he wanted her to be stunned when he knocked her socks off—as stunned as he'd been when she'd done the very same to him.

The second he reached for the buttons on her pajama top, Becky suspected Mack meant to turn the tables on her. He managed to undo every last one of them without ever letting his fingers touch her skin. The material parted only slightly, giving him a glimpse of smooth white skin, but still hiding the rounded flesh that ached for his touch.

When he didn't move to bare her to him at once, she knew she was right. He intended to tease her, torture her, turn her inside out, precisely the same way she had done to him.

He would watch her face for reactions to every move he made, smile wickedly at the half-pain, half-pleasure expression she knew she would give him. And he'd enjoy every minute of it.

Which was only fair. She'd driven all rational thought from his mind. Now he would do the same to her. She couldn't wait.

He started his journey at her shoulders, using his index fingers to trace twin lines downward, gliding past her collarbone and over the satin-covered tips of her breasts.

His fingertips converged at a point well below her belly button, but he halted before he touched her there, where she wanted him to, between her legs in the place that was needy, already hot, already aroused by what she'd done to him.

Bringing his hands back up to her waist he gripped her tightly. She rested her own hands on his shoulders, and he effortlessly lifted her until she was standing on the bed.

Leaning closer, he nuzzled her top aside with his face and used one finger to drag the waistband of her pajama bottoms just low enough to expose her tummy.

His tongue drew a circle around her navel, leaving a warm, moist ring in its wake. Then he exhaled, his warm breath hitting damp skin, sending a cool tingling sensation skittering over her abdomen and down her legs.

She gripped his shoulders with all her might, terrified she'd soon collapse in a heap. Too soon. With a desperation she didn't truly understand, she yearned to withstand the sweet agony as long as he had.

She doubted she would, though. She wasn't nearly so strong. And he was so very clever.

His mouth continued its assault, leaving wet, imaginative kisses over every inch of her belly as his hand slowly slid up the back of her leg and cupped her buttocks, holding her against him, forcing her to accept his erotic ministrations.

After an eternity, he slid her bottoms the rest of the way down her legs. Holding one of her hands to balance her, he slipped the garment over first one foot, then the other, before tossing it behind him with such gusto, it landed halfway to the bedroom door. The top joined the bottoms seconds later, leaving her standing before him on the bed wearing only a pair of skimpy bikini panties.

He gazed up at her, and she wondered if she looked as dazed with passion as he did, as his fingers toyed with the lacy edges of her panties. The thought that they were both so unbelievably excited gave her such a thrill, such a feeling of power, her knees nearly buckled. She held on to him, squeezing her hands around his biceps, willing his strength to flow up into her fingers and throughout her body to keep her upright.

That wasn't necessary, though, because he took her hand and pulled her down until she was once again seated on the edge of the bed. Clasping her knees in his hands, he eased her legs apart, spreading them wide, then knelt on the floor in front of her, letting her thighs cradle his torso.

Beginning at her knees, his hands traveled along her legs, then followed the inward curve of her waist upward until they were at the sides of her breasts. He used the pads of his thumbs to fondle her and tease her nipples into tight buds, then brought his head down and let his tongue test their nubby hardness.

A second later, he drew the sensitive peak into his mouth and suckled her.

She threw her head back and closed her eyes tightly, then arched her back, instinctively pressing herself more firmly against his lips, reveling in the feel of his wet tongue as it slid over her, around her.

It seemed like hours passed before he freed her aching flesh. Lifting her head she watched as he used one finger to slide her panties to the side until all her secrets were revealed to him.

She was so aroused, so ready for him, she wanted to cry; her feminine curls so damp with desire, he had to know that if he'd wanted to make her crazy with desire for him, he'd accomplished his goal.

For a long moment, he looked at her, touching her only with his eyes, seeming content to gaze at the precious part of her he would know intimately soon enough. Then, still holding her panties aside, he brought his other hand up and slowly slid one finger deep, deep inside of her.

Her head fell back again and she let out a moan of pleasure so long and loud, it shocked her.

"You're hot and wet and aching for more, aren't you?" he asked, his voice rough with passion and an unsatisfied need of his own.

"Yes. *Yes*," she exclaimed. "I need more. Please . . . *more*."

He rewarded her honesty at once, sweeping her panties down and off her body, allowing her to spread her legs so much wider for him.

As if he were handling a fragile orchid, his fingers carefully parted her delicate folds. She drew in an expectant breath, and after a seemingly endless moment, he brought his mouth down to her.

She knew at once she was in super deep trouble.

His lips and teeth and tongue would show even less mercy than his finger had, and it wouldn't be long before she was begging shamelessly for him to take her over the edge.

She didn't care.

Both her hands clasped fistfuls of his hair as he worked his magic on her with single-minded devotion.

"More," she cried. "I have to have it."

"What?" he asked, his voice barely above a whisper as he raised his head and looked up at her, a wicked smile on his lips. "What do you have to have?"

"All of it. I need *you*. Inside me . . . now," she added in a whisper, feeling a shocking lack of shyness as she confessed how much she needed completion, how much she needed him.

He shook his head. "No . . . not yet."

Falling back onto her elbows, she moaned again, wondering how much more she would be able to stand.

Slowly, he bent his head and placed his mouth against her once again. She sighed with relief, satisfied to have him at least touching her again, caressing her. But the feeling was fleeting, because within seconds, he had her wound tight, so feverishly tight, she knew she would burst any second.

As if sensing she was nearing the end of her endurance, he finally drew the tight nub of her desire into his mouth, sucking hard, harder, then swirling his tongue around and around the swollen peak, until she thought she would shatter into a million pieces.

A second later, she did.

Convulsive shudders wracked through her body as she climaxed, the feminine contractions coming one after another in fierce waves as he used his mouth to draw every last tremor from her quivering body.

When at last she was spent, her arms gave out and she fell back onto the bed, completely, utterly exhausted.

She heard the quiet rustle of the bed covers, then felt the bed dip with his weight as he knelt beside her on the mattress. He tenderly gathered her into his arms and lifted her, then resettled them both in the center of the bed and pulled the covers over them.

They lay together for several minutes. He held her tight, stroking her hair, whispering words of assurance as she dragged in huge gulps of air. She had no idea how much time passed before her breathing slowed, but eventually it did. Her pulse, which had felt like it was pounding uncontrollably, at last quieted to a steady, familiar pace.

She turned, angling her head back so she could meet his gaze. "I—"

She froze, not exactly certain what she'd been about to say. Jerking her head back down, she hid her face from his penetrating scrutiny, feeling suddenly, inexplicably . . . *shy*?

How could that be? It seemed like such an impossibly odd emotion for her to feel, given the intimacies they'd just shared. Or maybe this unexpected attack was *because* they had been so intimate. And because it had felt so right to share them with this man, in ways she never had with any other man.

"Beck?"

She burrowed her face in his naked chest, petrified he would be able to tell if he looked in her eyes that she had stumbled onto a significance to their actions that he might not find mutual. "What?" she mumbled.

"Look at me."

She shook her head, and her skin grazed his nipple. Hot need pierced through her as that same nipple constricted into a hard peak beneath her cheek.

Mack clenched his teeth, trying to ignore the strong desire her simple action ignited within him. He placed his hand beneath her chin and applied just enough pressure to force her to comply with his order.

"You're embarrassed, aren't you?" When she didn't answer him, he released a heavy sigh. "Please don't be," he told her, hoping his words came out sounding as sincere as he meant them to be. "It was beautiful, watching you come apart like that, knowing I was able to do that for you. The way you did for me," he added in a soft voice.

That seemed to get her attention. She raised up onto one elbow and frowned down at him, looking thoroughly confused.

"For you? But you didn't . . ." She blinked several times, then looked away. "I mean . . . we didn't actually . . . well, you know."

She turned a shade pinker with each attempt to

spell it out for him, and when she added a gesture to her explanation, it was—at best—a rough approximation of the act she was trying to describe.

He stared at her for a second, hardly able to believe what he was hearing. A few minutes earlier, she'd teased him to the point of exploding, taken him deep into her mouth and tortured him until he'd been damn near out-of-his-mind crazy with pleasure.

And now she couldn't even say the word climax. Or any appropriate euphemism.

He couldn't help it. He closed his eyes, sank his head deeper into the pillows beneath him, and laughed.

"What's so funny?" Before he could blink, she smacked his chest.

His eyes flew open in time for him to catch her indignant glare before she rolled away and buried her face in a pillow.

Absently rubbing the spot where she'd whacked him, he studied the smooth line of her narrow shoulders and naked back, followed the gently rounded curve of her lean hips to her legs, and all the way down to her feet and tiny toes.

Big things come in small packages, he thought, and the best example he'd ever seen of that age-old saying was lying right next to him.

A bit late, he realized his error. He never should have laughed at her tongue-tied explanation. Especially since he'd found it charming. Hell, he found her charming, and at the moment, he couldn't think of any good reason why he'd acted like such a jerk.

He only knew his insensitive behavior had hurt her—and that was the last thing in the world he'd wanted to do.

Hoping she wouldn't get more violent than that irritated slap, he slipped his arm around her waist and drew her back against him, tucking her naked behind up tight against his groin.

When she didn't push him away or execute any quick-but-deadly maneuvers, he decided to proceed.

"Becky?" he whispered, intentionally exhaling her name softly into her ear.

She shivered.

He smiled into her hair and took a chance on letting his hand glide over her hip. "Sweetheart?"

"What?" she asked in a belligerent, leave-me-alone, you-animal tone of voice.

"I wasn't laughing at you. I was—"

"Humph. Sounded like you were to me," she said, emphasizing her opinion with a quick backward thrust of her hips.

Mack grunted, even though he'd enjoyed her unique style of punctuation.

"Hey, I thought we'd agreed a man was innocent until proven guilty," he said, trying to sound insulted by her accusation.

Silence followed.

A long moment later, she wiggled her derriere in a maybe-I-did-jump-the-gun-and-sentence-you-to-life-without-parole-too-soon sort of way that told him he'd won the preliminary hearing.

His confidence buoyed, he snuggled closer. "I wasn't laughing at you," he repeated in a whisper. "I was charmed, fascinated, turned into putty by an unbelievably bright ray of sunshine named Rebekah."

The moment the words came out of his mouth, he realized he'd played the dirtiest trick of all on himself. He'd bared his soul. Completely and without censure, he'd told the honest-to-god truth about the way he felt about her.

He really was enchanted. There was no other way to explain the fact that he'd been acting crazy, out of character, breaking all his own hard-and-fast rules almost from the moment he'd met her.

The realization scared the hell out of him, but there wasn't a damn thing he could do about it.

For several minutes, Becky didn't move. He knew the exact moment she'd forgiven his abominable behavior, because he could feel the stiffness flow from her body. A second later, she turned in his arms to face him. Her eyes were big and blue and more beautiful than ever.

"You were really . . . charmed? You're not just

saying that 'cuz I slugged you." She smiled shyly as she brought her hand up and swept the hair back off his forehead.

"I really was," he said, and lowered his mouth to hers.

NINE

They didn't play any games this time.

There were no meaningful gazes, no suggestive inquiries, no whisper-soft caresses meant to drive a person out of his—or her—mind.

And there were no rules—save one: No holding back.

They each seemed to understand the silent edict. Each knew what they wanted, what they desperately had to have so very soon.

Mack held her delicate face in his hands as he assaulted her mouth, claiming possession of her lips with a fierce need that would have frightened him if he'd stopped to think about it.

He was taking, giving, demanding, receiving, aching, throbbing—experiencing all there was to experience, allowing no thought into his head that wasn't centered exclusively, erotically, on the woman lying beneath him.

He plunged his tongue deep into her mouth, ran his hands over her soft body, pulled her tight against him until they were fused together from chest to thighs, determined more than ever to have it all with her. Tonight.

She matched his aggressive actions with bold moves of her own, then pushed against his shoulders with both hands until she'd forced him onto his back.

Throwing one leg over his thighs to hold him in place, she climbed on top of him and straddled him. She placed her hands on his chest and locked her elbows, cradling his hardness between her womanly folds.

She gazed down at him, her breasts heaving with the effort it took to draw in much needed air.

"Now?" she asked him, waiting only a second for him to nod his head before lifting up and impaling herself on his waiting member.

She was so wet, so ready for him, he slid into her easily, sinking to the hilt so quickly, it took his breath away.

He froze momentarily, watching her, giving her body time to adjust to the delicious invasion she'd forced upon herself.

Her head was thrown back, her fingers gripping his biceps, her mouth curved into the sweetest, most contented smile he had ever seen.

He knew, at that moment, that he would never be able to get enough of her. She was everything he had avoided for six long years, and now, suddenly, everything he would crave for the rest of his life.

At first, Becky moved her body in a slow, steady rhythm. Up and down, side to side, around and around. But then she increased her pace with each new movement until she was sure they were both going to explode.

She let out a long, low groan, and before she could drag in another breath, he rolled her onto her back and plunged into her again. Deeply, repeatedly, harder and faster. Each powerful thrust took them that much higher, that much closer to the edge.

She wrapped her legs around him and clung to him, holding him tight, stunned by his strength, his control, his incredible skill. He'd brought her so far, so fast, and though she wanted this magnificent feeling to last forever, she couldn't hold out any longer.

Crying out his name, she dug her fingers into his back and catapulted into the universe untethered.

A moment later, Mack followed her.

❖━━━━━━━━━━━❖

Mack pumped his arms harder and lengthened his stride as he jogged past the picnic area at the south end of the city park, a few blocks from Becky's apartment.

Straight ahead in the distance he could see the sun trying to poke its nose up over the horizon, a bright yellow-white globe trying its damnedest to rise above the clouds.

He'd been running for more than forty-five minutes, and about a mile or so back it had occurred to him that maybe he should have left Becky a note telling her where he'd gone. He hadn't given it a thought when he'd left, probably because he wasn't used to having a woman wonder where he was the morning after—or care if he might be coming back anytime soon.

He'd simply retrieved his gym bag from the trunk of his car, pulled on his sweats, and hit the pavement, hoping to turn his predawn insomnia into an early-morning workout.

Who the hell are you trying to kid, Hoyle?

Who, indeed, he admitted silently, stepping up his pace. He'd gone running not because he'd felt some overwhelming need to expend energy or burn off stress, which was often the case when he resorted to such a vigorous routine at the *beginning* of his day, rather than the end.

No, he was out there before sunrise because the streets were quiet and deserted, and he needed to think.

Normally, Mack wasn't much of a Monday-morning quarterback. He didn't go over each and every move he'd made the day—or night—before in an effort to analyze, evaluate, figure out where he'd gone wrong.

But last night's events, he admitted as he zig-zagged his way around a pile of broken beer bottles, presented a different problem, one that deserved special consideration. Last night he hadn't blown a case or misinterpreted evidence or jumped the gun and arrested the wrong suspect.

No, he'd committed a crime that was much worse. A capital offense, according to his way of thinking. He'd gotten involved.

Seriously involved, he amended, knowing it wouldn't do any good to downplay the situation. He had to face the facts. Last night hadn't been just a one-night stand with a woman he didn't really care about. Last night had been the beginning of some sort of relationship, the sort he'd intentionally stayed clear of for six years.

So why'd you do it, buddy? And why'd you let yourself get involved with that particular woman?

A couple of real good questions, he acknowledged, absently giving a high-five to a patrol car as it rolled by him. He came up with an answer to the first one right away.

He couldn't help it. He'd tried to resist Becky, given it his best shot, then finally surrendered. And once he had, he'd been able to see he'd been fighting a losing battle all along. He just hadn't wanted to admit it. Or face the consequences.

The second question—why Becky?—was a bit more complicated to answer.

Immediately, memories of an unforgettable night spent making love to a bundle of contradictions swept over him.

Becky had aroused him and teased him and satisfied him as no woman ever had, all the while looking like she was hardly old enough to know the first thing about what went on between a man and a woman behind closed doors. But she'd known plenty.

She was sweet and naughty, shy and aggressive, remarkably innocent and oh-so-wild. She shocked the hell out of him one minute and turned bashful on him the next.

But he'd be shortchanging them both if he tried to convince himself he'd chosen her just because she'd given him the best sex of his life. She'd given him so much more.

In the short time he'd known her she'd given him peace of mind and taught him how to relax and smile again. She'd shown sympathy for the problems and frustrations he faced every day of his life, and offered him understanding and compassion as no one else ever had.

So, Hoyle . . . what have you given her?

That one stopped him dead in his tracks. Bent over at the waist, hands braced on his knees, he took in huge gulps of air as he tried to come up with something—anything—that he had given her. He came up empty.

Shaking his head in disgust, he straightened, then started off again, holding his pace down to a brisk walk. When he reached the entrance gate to the park, he exited and made a sharp left, heading back toward Becky's apartment.

Along the way, he made a decision. He didn't care what it took, he'd think of something he could give Becky that would even the score a bit.

The first thing Becky noticed when she woke up was that she was alone. Rolling onto her side, she reached for the pillow Mack had laid his head on throughout the night. She inhaled deeply, taking in the clean spicy scent of him that still lingered on the pillowcase.

They'd had such a wonderful night together, making love, telling silly jokes, whispering intimate secrets. Sometime in the early morning hours, they'd finally fallen asleep, totally exhausted, in each other's arms. And that was the way she'd expected to awaken—with his arms still around her.

Sitting up, she looked around the room, wondering if Mack had left without waking her. That thought vanished a second later when she realized the water in her shower was running. She let out a deep breath, surprised to discover how relieved she felt to know he was still there.

Had she really expected him to sneak off while she was sleeping?

She thought about that for a minute, then realized she didn't know what she expected where Mack was concerned. Things had happened so fast between them, she hadn't had a chance to consider the "morning after." And she didn't want to think about it now either. She just wanted to be with him and take one day at a time.

Tossing back the bed covers, she jumped from the bed, then stepped over a gym bag and pile of sweats on her way to the bathroom. He must have gone out for an early-morning run, she mused.

Through the steamed-up shower door, she made out the outline of his body and smiled, remembering in detail the hard lines and planes she'd become so familiar with the night before. The memory caused a pool of heat to gather low in her belly, and she couldn't wait another second to join him. Opening the shower door, she stepped inside.

"Finally decided to get your lazy butt out of bed?" he asked, smiling as he pulled her beneath the warm spray and into his arms. He brought his mouth down on hers and kissed her deeply. "I've been waiting in here so long, I was afraid I would run out of hot water before you joined me."

His body was covered with soapsuds. When he suggestively rubbed against her, their skin created a deliciously slippery friction, causing an immediate— and predictable—reaction.

She leaned far enough back in his arms to allow herself to peer down at him. Bringing her gaze back up to meet his, she said, "Looks like you could have used a cold shower." She laughed at his scowl.

"Is that the only cure you can think of for my condition?"

"I don't think there is a cure," she answered. As she slid her hands down his back and over the firm curves of his buttocks, the water streamed over their bodies and rinsed away the last of the soap.

"Oh yeah?"

Reaching behind him, he shut off the water, then picked her up in his arms, nudged the shower door open, and carried her back into the bedroom, heedless of the fact that they were still dripping wet.

He laid her down on the bed, climbed on top of her, and slid into her, burying himself so deep inside her, her breath caught in her throat.

Bracing his arms on either side of her, he pushed himself up and gazed down at her. "Still think there's no cure for what ails me?"

Nodding, she grinned up at him. "It's a chronic condition . . . and it'll just keep coming back."

He dipped his head and dropped a chaste kiss on the tip of her nose, then he partially withdrew and plunged back into her. "I know," he said, matching her smile. "That's what I like about it."

"Have you got the sports section over there by you?" Mack asked.

Becky watched him riffle through the pile of newspapers on the bed beside him and smiled, marveling at their good fortune.

In spite of the ungodly hours Mack had been putting in trying to solve the Denton case—along with so many others—they'd managed to spend three Sundays in a row together, sleeping in, enjoying breakfast in bed . . . enjoying each other.

"What do you have to offer in trade?" she asked, waving the coveted section in her outstretched hand.

Mack threw back the covers with a flourish. He held his arms out wide, grinning from ear to ear, not the least bit self-conscious about the fact that he was buck naked and fully aroused. Again. "Guess."

Laughing, she held her arm farther away. "Seems like an okay deal to me, but this time I insist you pay up *before* you get to read your precious sports news."

With lightning-fast speed, he rolled over and snatched the newspaper from her hand, then tossed it to the floor. He pulled her beneath him, crushing her breasts against his hard chest as he cradled his arousal between her thighs. "I was hoping you'd lay down the law."

His mouth came down on hers, nibbling at the corners before moving on to graze her earlobe with his teeth and tongue. The more she sought his mouth with hers, the more he teased, chuckling at her ineffective attempts as he planted soft kisses on her cheeks and neck and eyelids, everywhere but on her lips.

She loved this side of him, the playful side she'd seen increasingly more often when they were together. And they'd been together a lot in the last few weeks, she thought, for they'd fallen into an easy routine that seemed to work well for both of them.

Whenever Mack could get away for a short break in the afternoon, he would wait for her by her car after school. They would drive to a nearby restaurant for a snack and to catch up on the events of the day.

Most of the time he would encourage her to do all the talking by asking her about her students and classes. Occasionally, though, he'd mention a case he was working on or air his complaints about the legal system and all the red tape involved in bringing a criminal to justice. And because he knew she was still concerned for Arturo's sake, he would always bring her up-to-date on his efforts to track down Robert Bailey, efforts that had come up frustratingly empty so far.

They'd managed to spend most evenings together as well, sharing late dinners Becky had waiting on the stove, watching silly sentimental movies that invariably made her cry, making love until the early-morning hours, when Mack would get dressed and drive home to catch some sleep before having to report to work.

Though it always felt like their time together went by too quickly, she soon learned to accept the situation and make the best of it. That was why she hadn't complained the night before when he'd told her he wouldn't be able to make it back there the following night. But that didn't mean she wasn't curious about the way he'd be spending his evening.

Bringing her hands up and placing them on either side of his face, she stilled his wandering mouth and forced him to look at her.

"Tell me about this stakeout you're going on tonight. Is it dangerous?" she asked.

He grinned down at her, his gray eyes bright with mischief. "Only if I eat too many chili dogs and drink too much coffee. Then I could find myself in deep doo-doo."

She laughed, then socked him on the shoulder. "Be serious."

He braced his hands on either side of her head, then slowly slid down her body and took one nipple into his mouth, skillfully using his lips to coax it into a hard peak.

"I am serious," he said, lifting his head to gaze at her as he circled the hard nub with his tongue. "Have you ever been stuck in a car all night with a bad case of the—"

"Stop." She punched him again. "I don't want to hear all the gory details."

He shrugged a shoulder. "You asked," he said, then turned his attention to the other breast.

Though they'd never talked about it, she strongly suspected she was violating some unwritten rule by expressing her concern. The way he refused to give her a straight answer confirmed her suspicions.

She tapped him on his shoulder. "Mack?"

He lifted his head again. "What now?" he asked, rolling to his side and propping his head up with one hand. With the other, he drew a haphazard pattern down between her breasts and over her tummy, then let his fingers wander in and out of the curls between her thighs in a lazy manner that she was sure was meant to distract her from asking any more questions.

She turned on her side and faced him. Reaching down between their bodies, she grasped his arousal and gave a gentle squeeze to get his attention. "Just promise me you'll be careful, okay?"

His hand stilled. He looked into her eyes for a long moment, then he lowered his head, taking her mouth in a soul-deep kiss that sent shivers up and down her spine. Lifting his head once again, he moved closer, leaning into her intimate caress. "I'll promise you anything, Beck, if you'll just shut up and stop trying to distract me from earning my sports pages."

TEN

Becky turned the corner and pushed the magazine cart down the hospital corridor until she'd reached her destination, the Emergency Room lounge. Rolling the cart to a stop, she used her foot to set the safety break, then gathered a stack of magazines in her arms.

"Hey, if it isn't my favorite hospital volunteer."

Becky looked up to see Dr. Shifner leaning against the admittance desk. She smiled. "And if it isn't my favorite ER warrior. How are things going tonight?"

"Slow." He shook his head and put on a mournful expression. "We haven't had a decent stabbing or shotgun wound yet."

She laughed at his regretful tone of voice, knowing he'd be happy if he never had to treat another traumatic injury in his life, if it meant human beings had stopped trying to kill one another.

"Don't worry," she told him, trying to appear sympathetic. "The night is young."

His face brightened. "Ah, yes. There's still time . . ."

Rolling her eyes at his antics, she dismissed him with a wave and turned toward the lounge. She was halfway through the doorway when the double doors of the Emergency Room entrance burst open and two paramedics wheeled in a patient.

"Hey, Doc. Got a bleeder for you."

Dr. Shifner threw down the chart he'd been jotting notes on and rushed over to the gurney, snagging a pair of rubber gloves off the supply shelf on his way. He threw the blanket off the man.

"What's the story, fellas?" he asked as he quickly used scissors to cut the policeman's uniform shirt away from his chest so he could examine the injury.

"Gunshot wounds, close range, probably a .45. The cops were still looking for the weapon, told us the shooter ditched it in a trash can or something before he tried to get away."

The doctor issued a series of orders to the ER nurse and an orderly while he inspected the wound. "Any more on the way in?" he asked.

"Yeah, another cop. And the perp—but there's no hurry where he's concerned."

Dr. Shifner looked up without lifting his head. "Dead?"

"As a doornail," the paramedic replied.

Dr. Shifner nodded, then stood up straight. "Okay, this one's going to need surgery. Let's get him prepped for the OR right away." He stripped off the gloves and tossed them into the waste can nearby.

Watching from the doorway to the lounge, Becky clutched the pile of magazines to her chest, feeling like her feet were bolted to the floor.

There's no reason to panic, she told herself. Just because there'd been a shoot-out between some policemen and a criminal, that did not mean that Mack was involved. There were other officers out on the streets, looking for suspects. He wasn't the only one.

Slowly, she turned her back to the ER, determined to keep herself busy doing the job she was there to do. She'd taken one step into the lounge when she heard the loud bang of a stretcher hitting the doors of the entrance once again.

"Dammit, Crawford," a familiar voice complained. "It's just a flesh wound, and I don't need medical attention. If you weren't such a dumb jack—"

"That's enough out of you, Hoyle. The captain said to see that you let a doctor take a look at that arm, and he'd have my head on a platter if I didn't follow his orders to the letter."

The pile of magazines Becky had been holding hit the floor, scattering in all directions. She whipped around in time to see the uniformed officer who was pushing the gurney slap his hand on Mack's shoulder and, none too gently, shove his charge back down until he was lying flat again.

Mack let out a yelp, following it with a string of obscene comments questioning Crawford's ability to perform any task assigned to him.

"I love it when you talk dirty to me, you know that, Hoyle?" Crawford said as he darted a look around the ER. "Hey, I gotta tiger with a thorn in his paw. Can we get some help over here please?"

Even though she knew she had no business going anywhere near an Emergency Room patient, Becky moved forward. With each step she took, she told herself she had to appear calm—at least as calm as she'd seemed to be when she'd first seen Mack, standing in the middle of her classroom floor with blood dripping down his forehead.

But this time he's been shot! a voice inside her head screamed.

She drew in a deep breath and forced herself to ignore the differences between the damage that could be inflicted by a rock and a bullet.

When she reached Mack's side, she folded her

arms tightly in front of her to hide her trembling hands and attempted to look like she was mildly annoyed to encounter him there in the hospital.

"So, you couldn't keep yourself out of trouble, I see," she said, surprised to hear how steady her voice sounded.

Mack looked up and swore again. "What the hell are you doing here, Beck?"

As inconspicuously as possible, she glanced down at the tiny hole in his left sleeve. Reddish-brown stains were spattered around it. Blood. Her heart lurched. *Oh, God.* She took a deep breath and reminded herself the hole in his shirt was small. The wound would be too. Wouldn't it?

"I might ask you the same question, Detective," she said dryly, hoping she looked irritated, rather than alarmed.

"I just stopped by to get an enema." He tossed a dirty look at Officer Crawford. "I've got this pain in my a—"

"Please control yourself, Detective," Becky interrupted. "You're in enough trouble as it is." She was glad he was able to make a joke. It probably meant he wasn't hurt too badly. At least that's what she hoped it meant.

"Oh, yeah?" he challenged.

"Yeah," she said, her spirits buoyed further by his surly attitude. "I distinctly remember you promising me you'd be careful when you left my house this morning, but here you are—"

"This *morning*, huh?" Crawford inserted with a knowing snicker. "Now ain't that cozy. Sergeant Joe Friday and Florence Nightingale here—"

"Shut up, Crawford, or I'll break your face and make you even uglier than you already are." Mack started to rise to make good on his threat, but Crawford slammed him back down. Mack grunted, then let loose with a few more expletives.

"Pipe down, Hoyle, you're in no condition to break anything. Except maybe the Guinness record for the most swear words used in front of a lady. Pardon his French," Officer Crawford added, courteously tipping his uniform hat in Becky's direction.

She angled her head down and hid her smile behind one hand, knowing that Mack would not be amused to discover she'd found his acerbic exchange with the officer funny.

"And for your information," she explained, "I got a call from one of the other volunteers asking me if I could fill in for her tonight."

"Just my luck," he muttered. "The do-gooder would have to be here the one time I show up in ER."

"Well, pardon me for being a good citizen and doing my part to help out."

Even though she knew he must be striking out

because he was in pain, his rude remark stung. She turned to walk away, but he managed to snag her wrist. She looked down at his hand, then into his eyes. The slightly glazed look he gave her told her he was indeed in a great deal of pain, but she suspected he didn't want her to make a fuss about it.

"Becky, please. Don't go. I didn't mean to snap at you. We found Robert Bailey."

"That's great."

"Yeah, except he wouldn't surrender peacefully. There was a shootout and he was killed."

She looked away briefly. "I'm sorry."

He shook his head. "Don't be. He was scum. Anyway, we can close the case now, and Arturo and his family can get back to trying to live a normal life. The kid can even return to school tomorrow."

Before she could respond, Dr. Shifner approached.

"Okay, what's the problem with this one?" he asked.

"It's just a flesh—"

"The poor fool went and got himself shot—"

"Hold it!" Dr. Shifner held up both hands to stop Mack and Officer Crawford from simultaneously shouting their own versions of what had happened. "I'll figure it out for myself. Wheel him into the first cubicle," he told Crawford, and followed after them, leaving Becky behind.

She watched them take Mack away, feeling somewhat reassured by Dr. Shifner's manner. But once Mack was out of sight, her legs started shaking, and she couldn't help wondering how close he'd come to getting killed.

Lecturing herself that it wouldn't do anyone any good to get all worked up about what *didn't* happen, she took several deep breaths. Regardless of what had gone on out there that night, Mack was going to be all right. He was more angry than injured. She believed that. She really did.

Feeling better already, she decided to chalk up her delayed reaction to her surprise at seeing Mack laid out on a stretcher. Who wouldn't get a little weak in the knees after a scare like that? she thought as she went back into the lounge and gathered up the magazines she'd dropped. But it was over now. Nothing to get excited about.

After placing the magazines on the end tables where they belonged, she retrieved her cart and wheeled it back down the hall to where it was stored. By the time she was through checking out with the volunteer office, she felt that she had calmed down considerably.

When she returned to the ER area, Mack was still in with Dr. Shifner, so she went into the lounge to wait for him.

Officer Crawford was sitting in a chair over

by the window. He stood up when she entered. "Ma'am."

She nodded. "Officer. Are you waiting for Detective Hoyle?"

"Yes, ma'am. I was told to make sure he goes straight home after he's done here."

She remembered Crawford's earlier remark about following his captain's orders to the letter. "I would be more than happy to take that job off your hands, Officer. That is, if you think I'm up to the task."

He hesitated, looking down as he fiddled with his hat. When he looked up again, he was grinning. "I guess you can probably handle him. But don't let him give you any guff about having to go file reports or nothing. The captain was real firm about that."

She pursed her lips and tried to look firm. "Absolutely no paperwork. I understand."

At the door to the lounge, Crawford paused to put his hat on, then turned back to face her. "Straight home, right?"

She smiled. "Yes, sir."

After he left, she went over to the couch and sat down, thinking it shouldn't be too much longer before the doctor was done with Mack. A minute later she stood up again and began to pace.

Why was it taking so long to treat a minor wound? she wondered. She shot an impatient glance at her watch, then let out a nervous laugh. It had only been ten minutes since they'd brought him in. It felt like hours.

Selecting a magazine from the batch she'd delivered earlier, she went back over to the couch. She forced herself to concentrate on reading an article instead of listening to the ticking of the clock on the wall.

"Beck?"

She jerked her head up to see Mack standing in the doorway to the lounge. She wondered how long she'd been sitting there, then wondered how long he'd been standing there watching her. She jumped up and hurried over to him.

"Are you all right?" she asked, hoping her concern had come through in her voice—but not the worry. Mack's evening had been bad enough already. It wouldn't help him any for her to fall apart on him.

Mack didn't answer her right away. Instead, he searched her face and body for signs of stress.

He thought she looked a little pale, but everyone did in the glaring lights they had in the hospital. Her eyes were clear, not overly bright the way they would have been if she'd been holding back tears, and she didn't seem to be trembling.

Her voice hadn't shook either when she'd asked him if he was all right, and she wasn't fidgeting nervously or fussing with him.

All the while the doctor had been bandaging his wound, he'd been wondering how she was taking his getting shot, wondering if she was beside herself with worry. But she seemed to be okay.

"The doctor says it's just a scratch," he finally said, marveling once again at her ability to surprise him. Every time he thought he had her pegged, she fooled him.

She smiled. "I'm glad to hear that."

"But I think I'm going to need some special attention right away," he said, his own smile suggestive.

She reached up and gave him a nice, deep, openmouthed kiss. "Let me guess . . . you need me to kiss it and make it better."

He pulled her closer with his good arm, planting his hand on her fanny as he rubbed his lower body against hers, making it impossible for her to miss the way he responded so quickly to her.

"Kiss what and make it better?" he whispered into her ear.

She threw her head back and laughed again. "Anything you want, Detective. But it could be a delicate, time-consuming operation, and I think we'd better find somewhere else to administer the treatment."

"Good idea." He lifted his head and looked around. "What happened to that pain in the butt Crawford?"

"I talked him into letting me take you home."

Mack grinned. "Oh, yeah?"

She nodded. "Any objections?"

He shook his head slowly. "Let's go home."

Mack felt his way through the darkened doorway of Becky's bedroom and headed down the hall. He'd awakened moments earlier to find himself alone in her bed. A glance at the clock on her bedside table had revealed it was after four A.M., and he'd wondered how long he'd been sleeping without her. Minutes? Hours?

When he reached the arched doorway to the living room, he paused. A pale yellow beam from a streetlamp filtered in through the rose curtains, providing the illumination he needed to make out the slight figure huddled in the chair by the window. Becky.

Her arms were wrapped around her legs and she was hugging them tightly against her chest, her chin resting on her knees. An old memory that he couldn't quite place tugged at him, making him feel oddly uncomfortable with the picture she made sitting there alone in the dark.

Feeling more and more uneasy with the shadowy recollection, he decided to go to her and bring her back to bed with him right away. He'd taken one step into the room when she turned her head slightly and her face caught the light. Seeing the glistening of tears on her cheeks, he froze.

The hazy memory came rushing back full force, and his heart plummeted to his stomach. Becky was crying, just like his mother had the first time his father had been shot. And Becky had hid her true feelings about it from him the same way as well.

He gripped the doorway with both hands to keep from pounding out his anger and frustration. He wanted to scream, but his mouth was too dry, his throat too tight to allow any sound past his lips.

How could he have been so *blind*? He should have known she would be tied in knots with worry after seeing him wheeled into the ER with a bullet wound in his arm. How could he have taken her calm reaction at face value?

Because he'd seen only what he wanted to see, heard only what he wanted to hear, and he'd been doing that since the day he'd met her.

He'd broken all the rules every step of the way with her, never giving a thought to how things would work out in the end. Now *she* was the one paying the price for his foolishness.

How could he have done that to her? How could he have been such a selfish bastard? She'd given him so much, and the only thing he'd managed to give her in return was a broken heart.

He felt a sharp stab of pain in his own heart as

he realized there was one other thing he could give her. A person as good and kind as Becky deserved more out of life than to spend every day worrying if this would be the day he got his fool head shot off. And worry she would. She wouldn't be able to stop herself. She'd already told him as much when she'd revealed how she worried about her parents.

But he knew he'd never be able to convince her it was for her own good that she stop seeing him. She'd stick out that stubborn chin of hers and dig in her heels, and before he would know what happened, she would have convinced him she was strong enough to withstand anything.

And it was true. She was. But it was equally true that she deserved better. He would have to see that she got it.

Knowing he had no choice, he took a calming breath, then walked over to where she sat and knelt down by her side.

"Come to bed, Becky," he said quietly.

"Mack?" She looked shocked to see him, frightened even. Hastily, she tried to wipe the tears from her face. "I wasn't really . . . I mean, I didn't want you to see me—"

"Shhh, baby. Don't cry." He ran the back of his hand over her cheek, his knuckles gliding over her smooth wet skin. "Everything's going to be okay."

"I'm sorry." Her shoulders sagged as if she were

relieved to have her feelings out in the open. "I tried to be brave. I really did. But after you fell asleep, I lay there with your arms around me, listening to you breathe, and I just started thinking about how awful it would be if you'd really been hurt badly. I don't know what I would have done," she cried, throwing her arms around his neck.

He stood up, lifting her into his arms. "Shh. You don't have to worry about that." *Ever again.*

"I couldn't stand to see you hurt," she whispered against his neck.

Don't worry. You won't ever have to.

He carried her into the bedroom and stood her on the floor next to the bed. He slowly untied the sash of the short robe she was wearing, then slipped the robe from her shoulders.

He looked at her for a long moment, drinking in her beauty. Her slender shoulders, her lovely round breasts, her tiny waist. Her skin was so soft, so smooth. She was so perfectly formed, he thought she really must be an angel.

"Mack?" She gazed up at him, her eyes filled with love, and he knew he'd made the right decision to give her her freedom. It would be the hardest thing he'd ever done in his life, but the most generous as well.

Before he did, though, he would selfishly take one more thing from her, the only thing he would have left of her. The only thing that might help him retain his sanity when the pain of losing her got to be too much.

He'd take memories. Of her, of them, of their last night together.

"Yes, Becky," he said as he picked her up. "I'm going to make love to you."

He laid her down on the bed, then stretched out next to her. Drawing her into his arms, he held her close for a long while, stroking his hands over her body with infinite tenderness. He caressed her arms and back, ran his fingers lightly over her hips and down her legs before retracing his path back her shoulders, committing each lovely line and curve to memory.

Gently, he rolled her onto her back and covered her body with his own, wanting with all his heart to remember the exact way they fit together so beautifully.

He worshiped her with his mouth, his tongue, his body, giving her all the pleasure she deserved, reveling in the sounds of satisfaction she made that told him he was pleasing her.

He paid special attention to the tiny hollow at the base of her neck, the firm lines of her collarbone, her flat stomach, the backs of her knees, the extrasoft skin on the insides of her thighs. Her peach-scented perfume seemed to be everywhere he touched as he used all his skill to work her into a feverish state of pure desire.

Her hands gripped the bedclothes, hanging on so tight, her knuckles turned white. She writhed beneath him, pleading with him to come inside her. He resisted her invitation for as long as he could, wanting, needing this final time to last as long as possible.

When finally he sensed she could stand no more of the exquisite torture he was treating her to, he lifted her hips and plunged into her warm body.

He held himself perfectly still for one long moment, treasuring the feel of her surrounding him, holding him tightly within her, caressing him tenderly with her inner muscles.

Then he began to move, slowly at first, sliding in and out in a lazy rhythm that teased them both, then faster and faster still. With each thrust, she cried out his name as he took them higher and higher. She gripped his shoulders and lifted her head off the pillow, seeking his lips.

He devoured her mouth, plunging his tongue deep within as he brought them closer to the moment of release, until he finally lost control. With one last hard thrust, he took them over the edge. They climaxed together, her muscles contracting around him, drawing every last spasm from him until he was exhausted and spent.

He collapsed on top of her, then rolled to his side, taking her with him, wrapping his arms tightly around her, holding her as close as he possibly could. Her breathing still labored, she snuggled into his heat. With one hand he snagged the covers and covered both of them.

Soon he felt her breath feathering over his chest in even waves, telling him she'd fallen asleep. He remained wide awake, wanting to savor every second of their last moments together. He knew he'd never have such peace or contentment ever again.

Shortly before dawn, he slipped out of bed, careful not to wake her, then quietly pulled on his clothes and walked out the front door, closing it softly behind him.

ELEVEN

Becky inched her way down Belmont Avenue before pulling her car over to the curb and putting it in park. Bracing one arm on the back of the seat, she bent over and peered out the passenger window, staring hard at the house directly in front of her.

"Middle of the block. Green shutters on either side of the kitchen window. Yep, this is the place," she said, thankful she'd been paying attention when Colleen Hoyle had described the house she lived in.

Straightening in her seat, Becky leaned back, gripping the steering wheel. It had been a week since Mack had been shot, a week since they made sweet, sweet love. And it had been just as long since she'd awakened alone and confused in the big brass bed she'd inherited from her maternal grandmother.

By her calculations, that added up to seven full days' worth of worry, unreturned telephone messages, and unanswered notes left on his front door.

Obviously, Mack was avoiding her, and he was doing an excellent job of it. The question was— why?

She suspected it had something to do with her delayed reaction to his getting shot. Though he hadn't said so at the time, she could tell he'd been greatly troubled at having found her sitting in her living room in the middle of the night, crying.

But was that reason enough for him to sneak out of her bed the following morning without saying a word, reason enough to disappear for days on end? And how long did he intend to stay away? Forever?

She wanted answers to those questions and a few others as well, and she was willing to play detective herself in order to track down the man who could give her those answers.

First thing on her agenda was to have a talk with Mack's mother. Becky figured she could use a few pointers on how to deal with a hardheaded man. Since Colleen had told her Mack and his father were a lot alike, Colleen was bound to be able to give Becky some much needed advice on how to handle Mack—when she finally caught up with him.

She ordered the butterflies in her stomach to

calm down, got out of her car, and walked up to the Hoyle house. Colleen answered the door immediately.

"Becky?" she said, naturally surprised to see Becky on her doorstep.

"I'm sorry for stopping by uninvited, but it's important that I talk to you, and I was hoping you wouldn't mind."

"Well, no." She shot a glance over her shoulder. "Of course not. Please . . . come in." Colleen led her into the kitchen. "I hope it's all right if we talk in here. I was just getting some dinner ready . . ."

"If I'm interrupting—"

"Not at all. I've already eaten, but I always serve—"

"Well, well. Doesn't this make a cozy picture. My mother and my latest paramour having a little chitchat."

Becky whipped her head around at the sound of that voice. "Mack?"

He was standing at the top of a stairway that emptied out into the far end of the kitchen, wearing a pair of jeans that rode low on his hips and nothing else. Though his face was partially shadowed by the sloped ceiling above his head, it was nevertheless obvious he hadn't shaved in days.

Until that moment, Becky hadn't realized how incredibly hungry she'd been for the sight of him, even if his disappearing act had made her so angry, she wanted to strangle him.

She watched him weave his way down the stairs, one hand gripping the oak banister while the other negligently waved a half-full beer mug in the air. Beer sloshed over the rim with every other unsteady step.

"Mackenzie Hoyle, in the flesh," he said, spreading his arms wide. "So to speak," he added, slurring his words enough that she could tell this wasn't his first beer of the evening.

Colleen's gaze locked on her son, then drifted to Becky, then back to her son. Without saying another word, she went over to the stove and ladled some soup into a bowl. She set the bowl on a serving tray with a napkin and silverware and carried it to the bottom of the stairway.

"I'll be upstairs," she said to no one in particular.

Mack nodded, then came the rest of the way into the kitchen and plopped down in a chair. "So . . ." He stretched his legs out in front of him. "What all-important business brings you to this neighborhood?"

Becky walked over to the table and sat down. "How's your arm?" she asked, ignoring his sarcastic tone.

He flexed his shoulder. "Just dandy, as a matter of fact."

"I'm glad to hear it. I was worried about you."

He planted one hand in the middle of his chest and gave her a look of surprise. "*Me?*"

She nodded. "I've called your house, left messages for you at the station, notes on your front door."

He took a sip of beer. " 'Fraid I haven't been home in a while. I've been hanging out over here since the captain made me take a leave of absence."

"I see." She looked away. "You left without saying good-bye."

He belched, then chased it with another swig of beer. " 'S'cuse me."

"Why?"

He drew his eyebrows into a frown. "Because it's bad manners to burp in front of a lady."

Becky clenched her teeth in frustration. This was a Mack she didn't recognize. She'd seen him tipsy the night of their picnic, and she'd seen him surly the night he'd been shot, but she'd never seen him tipsy and surly at the same time. It was a nasty combination, one she wasn't sure how to deal with.

She lifted her chin, deciding the best thing to do was appear as though his rude behavior didn't faze her. "I mean, why did you leave?"

He shrugged. "It seemed like the best thing to do at the time."

"I don't understand."

"What's to understand? It wasn't going to work out between us, so I split. Okay?"

She shook her head, unable to believe what she was hearing. "No, it's not okay. We made *love* the last time we were together. You were kind and gentle and caring. It was the most beautiful—"

He slammed his mug down on the table, cutting her off in midsentence. "Let's just skip the walk down Memory Lane, shall we? I'm not in the mood. Besides, like I said a minute ago, it's not going to work out between us, and if you'd take off those damn Pollyanna glasses you're always wearing, you'd be able to see that."

Becky flinched. It had been a while since she'd encountered Mack the Cynic, and she'd almost forgotten how hard and negative and . . . irritating he could be.

Still, her heart went out to him. Whatever was bothering him must be more serious than she'd imagined. She figured the only way she'd be able to get through to him would be to confront him directly.

"Does this have something to do with your getting shot?" she asked.

He let out a bark of laughter. "You mean, does this have something to do with me almost getting myself *killed*?"

She sucked in a breath and held it for a long moment before letting it out. "It was a flesh wound. You said so yourself."

"It could have been worse."

"But it wasn't," she said calmly, even as she relived the panic she'd felt in the Emergency Room, wondering how close he'd come to getting killed.

Slowly, Mack got to his feet and walked over to the kitchen sink. Facing the window, he braced his hands on the tile counter and let his head fall forward, then blew out a frustrated sigh.

The second he'd seen her standing in the kitchen, he'd realized how very much he'd wanted to see her again. For a moment, he'd allowed himself the selfish luxury of remembering all the things he'd missed since he'd slipped out her door—seeing her smile, holding her close, making love to her for hours on end.

He shook his head viciously, trying to clear his mind of the images he had no business dwelling on, willing his brain to concentrate on what was important.

For days now, he'd been hoping she wouldn't try to find him, praying she'd recognize him for the jerk he was for leaving her the way he did and decide he wasn't worth the trouble.

He should have known better. He should have realized Becky would never think the worst—even of the bastard who'd made love to her one minute and ducked out on her the next.

No, Becky would never give up on a person that easily. She believed in people—believed in *him*. Even when presented with the cold hard evidence that proved he didn't deserve her faith.

He turned around to face her. "What about the next time?" he asked. "What if I get hurt a whole lot worse? What then?"

She stood up. "Mack, just because you got shot once doesn't mean it will happen again."

"Becky, I'm a cop. A *homicide* cop. The bad guys I'm after are *murderers*. They carry guns, knives, lethal weapons of every shape and size imaginable."

She walked over to him, stopping directly in front of him. "What are you trying to tell me, that you're in danger every day of your life? Don't you think I know that?"

"I think you do now, because that reality finally hit home when they wheeled me into the Emergency Room with a bullet hole in my arm."

Biting down on her lower lip, she turned her head away. When she finally brought her eyes back to his, they were brimming with tears.

"I know what this is all about, Mack. You saw me crying, and now you think I can't handle your job."

"You're absolutely right. I don't."

"Well, you're wrong. I was upset, yes, but what

do you expect? I've never been in that situation before." She swiped at her face with the back of her hand, smearing tears across her cheeks. "I love you—"

"Don't—"

"I love you," she repeated. "And I was concerned," she added in a whisper.

Pain slammed into him, as sudden and shocking as the one caused by the bullet he hadn't been able to dodge a week ago.

She loved him. He told himself her actions had been demonstrating that for some time, that it shouldn't make a bit of difference now that he'd heard her say the words. But it did, and he felt his resolve weaken. "Oh, Becky—"

"Please don't be angry with me. I've never seen the man I love hurt like that before." She gave him a little half smile that he was sure was meant to make him think she was doing fine.

But he'd seen the way her bottom lip quivered, and it took every ounce of strength he had to keep from pulling her into his arms to comfort her. He hated what this was doing to her, hated that he had to hurt her so badly to make her understand, but he didn't see any other way.

"I'm not angry," he said without raising his voice, determined not to lose control and contradict himself.

Her eyes questioned his. "Why else would you have left the way you did? Why else would you have stayed away from me so long?"

Suddenly, he snapped. He grabbed her by the arms and shook her. "Because I'm trying to protect you!" he shouted. "Can't you see that? This is no life for you. You deserve better."

"I deserve to be with you. No matter what."

No matter what. She could say that, he told himself, only because she had no idea what horrors the future might have in store for them. But he did. He had a very good idea, and he hated the thought of her ever being forced to share such a future with him.

"Becky, please," he pleaded. "Don't make me tell you—*show* you—how bad it could be. Just leave." Feeling defeated, he released her and pushed her away from him.

Becky stood perfectly still as she watched Mack struggle with his emotions. She loved him so much. She loved his tough-guy exterior and the way he turned to mush when she cried. She loved the man who trusted no one and the man who cared enough about people to risk his life to protect and serve them. She loved the son who was concerned enough about his mother to feel real pain when he caused her to suffer.

She stepped closer. Taking his face in her hands, she pressed her lips to his. "I love you, Mack, and nothing you could ever say or do would make me want to leave you."

Mack knew she hadn't meant to make her words sound like a challenge. But in a sense, that's exactly what they were, and he really had no choice but to prove to her that she was wrong.

He took her hand and led her toward the stairs. "Come with me," he said, hating himself for doing this to her, but knowing no other way to convince her she was better off without him.

Becky followed him up the stairway and down the hall. When he came to the last room on the right, he paused and turned toward her.

"I wish . . ." He shook his head, then pulled her into the doorway. Placing his hands on her shoulders, he stood behind her, angling her toward the center of the room.

Colleen was sitting in an armchair by the side of a large hospital-style bed, newspaper in hand, reading out loud to the man lying in the bed. They seemed unaware of Becky and Mack's presence.

Becky stood there listening to Colleen rattle off the final scores to last night's basketball games, taking in the peaceful scene for a few minutes before she realized what she was seeing. Then the truth hit her.

The man appeared to be at least sixty years old. His pale skin was paper thin, seeming to cling to an emaciated frame that looked silly taking up so little space in that giant bed. Chocolate-brown hair shot through with gray trailed along the top of his head and over his ears, a few stray wisps falling down across his forehead.

The upper third of the bed was elevated to a forty-five-degree angle. When the man's head lolled over to one side, seemingly of its own volition, Becky finally got a glimpse at his eyes. Focused on nothing in particular, they were clear and gray and stunningly identical to another pair she knew so well.

She looked over her shoulder to meet Mack's unwavering stare, then slowly turned back to the man in the bed.

"Rebekah de Bieren, I'd like you to meet my father, Sergeant Joseph P. Hoyle." Mack let out a snort. "Pretty pathetic, huh?"

Becky covered her mouth to keep from crying out at the harsh, unyielding tone of Mack's voice. When she tried to meet his gaze once again, he jerked his head to the side, but not before she saw the pain in the depths of his eyes.

At that moment, she sensed someone looking at her, and turned to see Colleen staring at them. Becky made eye contact with Colleen for only a second before Colleen went back to reading the paper to Joseph.

"About all he can do is lie there," Mack continued, still refusing to look at her. "That and drool. But he's got that mastered pretty well—"

Becky put her hands over her ears to shut out the horrible things he was saying.

"Stop it," she whispered, shooting a glance in Colleen's direction, hoping she hadn't heard Mack. "Just stop it!"

Then she turned and ran.

"Well, I guess that takes care of that," Mack muttered, then closed the door and went back downstairs.

"That was a rotten thing to do, Mackenzie."

Mack raised his head from his hands to see his mother standing at the bottom of the stairs, a pile of newspapers in her arms. "What are you talking about?"

She walked over and placed the papers with the others in the bin for recycling, then came over and stood in front of him. "You never told her about your father's condition. You just took her up there to meet him without any warning."

"She had to learn the truth sometime."

"Not that way, she didn't." Shaking her head, Colleen laid a hand on his shoulder. "Oh, Mack, what could you possibly have been thinking to have done such a thing?"

He shrugged off her concern and stood up. "You want to know? I'll tell you. I was thinking that she ought to see what she might have to look forward to if she decides she wants to spend her life with a cop." He grabbed his shirt off the back of the chair and put it on, ignoring the buttons. "She could get to bathe him and spoon-feed him and change his diapers and wipe the spittle from his chin a hundred times a day. In fact, she could get to be just like *you*."

Colleen sat down in the chair Mack had just vacated. "Would that be so bad?" she asked, her voice taking on a confrontational quality he found surprising.

"Yes. You spend every day and night of your life taking care of a man who can't do the simplest thing for himself. Becky deserves better." As soon as the words left his mouth, he realized what it sounded like he was implying. He rushed over to his mother and knelt down in front of her, taking her hands in his. "*You* deserve better too. This is no life for you."

"It's the life I chose."

"No, it isn't. You were barely twenty years old and eight months pregnant when Dad came home and announced he was joining the police force. There wasn't much you could do but go along with him on it."

"Don't kid yourself, Mackenzie. I'm a strong woman. If I'd wanted to leave your father then, I would have, and I would have found a way to make a good life for you and me." She patted his hand, taking the sting out of her rebuke. "But I loved your father, and I chose to stay and share this life with him."

Mack stood up again. He shoved his bare feet into his shoes, then snatched his house keys off the table. "Fine, but I don't want Becky making that choice."

"I'm afraid this isn't about what you want, son. It's about what she wants. In case you haven't noticed, these days women like to make their own decisions."

"That's too bad. I made this one for her. Now she doesn't have to worry about one day getting stuck with the booby prize."

Colleen shook her head and smiled wistfully. "I wish there was some way I could make you understand it isn't such a horrible choice. I had over thirty wonderful years with your father before his accident."

"And what about the last six years? How have they been?"

She tipped her head to one side and looked up at him. "Different, I'll admit. But they've been wonderful in their own way, because we've been together, your father and I. Maybe he can't walk and talk and take care of himself like he used to, but he understands me when I talk to him. And he knows I love him."

Mack walked over to the door and put his hand on the knob. "That's the problem, Mom. You love him too much."

He was halfway out the door before he heard her voice again. "I never figured you for a coward, Mackenzie."

Coward?

He whipped around to ask her what the hell she was talking about, but she'd left the room.

Becky didn't know how she made it home from Colleen Hoyle's house in one piece, but she did.

With tears swimming in her eyes, she drove herself across town, trying not to think.

Once seated at her kitchen table, a cup of hot chocolate in front of her, she started to piece together bits of information that might help her unravel the confusion of what had occurred that evening. She began with the most shocking piece of the puzzle—Joseph Hoyle.

At first, she'd thought Mack had lied to her when he'd told her his father was no longer alive. But then she'd recalled his exact words—we lost him six years ago—and realized he'd never actually said the man was dead.

She picked up her mug and used her tongue

to swipe the marshmallow floating on top of the chocolate. He'd only led her to believe that was the case, she reminded herself. He'd never intended for her to find out he'd purposely given her the wrong impression.

On a roll, she found herself remembering snatches of conversations they'd had when they'd first started seeing each other, specifically all the warnings he'd issued.

If you have so much as an ounce of self-preservation in you . . .

You should get the hell out of here while you still can . . .

You don't have any idea what you'd be getting into if you got involved with me . . .

Now that she knew the truth about Joseph—the whole truth, including the fact that Colleen obviously took care of him every day—Becky could see why Mack had been so determined to discourage her from getting involved with him. Although the possibility might be slim, he'd known that what had happened to his father *could* happen to him.

He'd been trying to protect her from ever having to deal with such a heartbreaking situation. And though she wished he'd had more faith in her ability to cope, she loved him for showing such concern for her welfare.

But she *had* gotten involved with him, and things

had been fine between them—until the night he was shot.

The night she'd cried and told him she didn't know what she would have done if he had been hurt, *really* hurt. When she'd told him she wouldn't have been able to stand it.

So once again, he was trying to protect her—and this time it was pathetically easy to understand why he would think she needed protecting. After all, a man who practiced cynicism as though it were a religion would naturally think a woman who'd come unglued over a minor gunshot wound would be totally incapable of dealing with the sort of circumstances his mother had to face each and every day.

But shedding tears because she realized the man she loved had been in mortal danger did not mean she needed to be protected and treated as if she were a child. She was a woman, and some women cried when they were upset. She was one of them, but that didn't mean she wasn't strong enough to handle anything she had to. There had to be some way to get that through the thick skull of one Mackenzie Hoyle.

Her brows furrowed in concentration, she sipped her hot chocolate and decided she'd just have to come up with a plan.

TWELVE

"Buddy, you look like hell."

Mack braced his hands on the bathroom counter and forced himself to look at the ugly mug staring back at him from the mirror above the sink.

His eyes were puffy and bloodshot from lack of sleep. He hadn't eaten a decent meal since he'd walked out of his mother's house three days ago, and hard as he tried, he couldn't remember the last time he'd showered or shaved.

His oily hair was matted to his head in some places, sticking straight in the air in others, and the shirt and jeans he'd been wearing nonstop for the last hundred or so hours were wrinkled and filthy and stank to the heavens.

In short, he was a god-awful mess, every bit as

repulsive as the poor bastards he shook his head in disgust at each time he passed by the drunk tank down at the precinct house.

"Keep this up, pal, and you won't have to worry about thinking of a way to get Becky to take your sorry butt back. You'll be dead."

It was the truth, he acknowledged, letting his head fall forward. Something he'd told precious little of lately. In fact, he'd spent the entire medical leave his captain had insisted he take feeling sorry for himself, wasting away, telling lies.

And until the moment Becky had shown up at his mother's place three days ago, he'd actually managed to convince himself he was getting away with it.

Shaking his head, he let out a derisive chuckle. He'd told some real whoppers, all right. And the biggest?

He'd told himself he could live without Becky. But he'd proved that was a bunch of bull over and over.

For the first time in a week and a half, he raised his head, stared himself straight in the eyes without blinking, and forced himself to be honest.

This wasn't living. It was existing, at best, which was about all he'd been doing before he'd met Becky. Back then, he'd spent his time working and jogging and working some more. If he wasn't on police business or jogging to forget police business, he was sleeping—fitfully.

He'd allowed himself to get so far out of touch with the rest of the human race, he'd begun to believe that everyone was a suspect or a snitch or a liar or a murderer. He'd become hard and cynical and downright humorless. A real fun guy.

Becky had been the one ray of sunshine in his sorry excuse for a life—and he'd been a fool to let her go.

He'd been an even bigger fool for believing that the reason he'd done so was for her sake.

He hung his head again. His mother was right when she'd accused him of being a coward. He'd been too damn afraid to let Becky love him so much that she'd stick by him the way his mother had stuck by his father.

When you love somebody, you take the good with the bad. It's a package deal.

Becky's words came back to him for at least the hundredth time, but this time he finally got the message.

How could he have been blind enough to think he was protecting *her* from the possibility of having to face the bad times? All along he'd been protecting himself, telling himself he'd rather be alone for the rest of his life than let someone share the risks.

Slowly, he raised his head and looked in the mirror again. This time, instead of just seeing his own reflection, he could have sworn he saw Becky standing behind him.

He whipped around, looking for her. He was alone.

But not for much longer, dammit.

Reaching into the shower, he gave the faucet a hard yank, turning the cold water on. He stripped off his clothes, stepped under the shower head, and yelled when the icy spray caught him square in the face.

Becky stood in front of the full-length mirror on her closet door and gave herself another once-over, still trying to decide if she'd managed to achieve the effect she was after.

Dressed to kill.

That was the phrase the saleslady had used when she'd sold Becky the crepe off-the-shoulder wonder, with its shirred, stand-away sleeves, sweetheart bodice that dipped real low in the front—and back— flared midcalf skirt that flowed out into a wide arc when she twirled in a circle. And the color—red for *passion*.

She'd spent the better part of three afternoons, combing the specialty boutiques for precisely the right thing to wear, and until a few minutes ago, she'd thought she'd succeeded. Now that it was time to put that plan into action, however, she was having doubts.

What if it didn't work? What if Mack took one look at her and thought she'd decided to moonlight as a lady of the evening and sent the vice squad after her?

Her shoulders sagged. Maybe it was a stupid idea, she thought, suddenly feeling foolish for having wasted so much time and money on a silly scheme to make Mack see her as a woman.

Lady of the evening? Hmphh. Even in this come-and-get-me number she looked like a little kid playing dress up.

She wasn't, though. A little kid, that is, and now that she thought about it, Mack was the one who'd shown her that was true. In spite of that overprotective streak of his, no man had ever made her feel more like a woman.

No man had ever inspired her to *act* more like a woman either, she thought, feeling her cheeks grow warm with the memory of their erotic, no-holds-barred lovemaking.

Straightening her shoulders once again, she took another look in the mirror. This time she saw a determined woman, one who loved a man enough to fight for him.

Grabbing the red-beaded purse she'd selected at the last minute to complete her outfit, she marched to the door with her head held high.

"Look out, Detective Hoyle," she said aloud. "You're about to meet your match."

Feeling invincible, she grabbed hold of the doorknob and threw open the door.

"Becky?"

"Mack?"

He stood with his right hand raised, as if he'd been about to knock on her door. He was wearing stone-washed blue jeans and a deep blue twill shirt under a nubby, natural-style silk sport coat. In his left hand, he carried a large brown paper sack. His gaze raked over her from head to toe and back again.

"Yeah, it's me," he said, forcing the words out between lips drawn into a tight line. "Who were you expecting, Mel Gibson?"

One look at the jealous rage burning in his steel-gray eyes and she knew the outrageous price she'd paid to achieve this sexy, knock-em-dead look had been worth every penny.

"Actually," she said, "I read in *People* magazine that he's shooting a movie on location somewhere in Canada right now." She loved the way her words came out sounding smooth and matter-of-fact. In reality, she felt as if the entire U.S. Olympic Basketball Team had taken to the court for practice—inside her tummy.

"Cute, Beck. Real cute. May I come in? Unless you *are* expecting someone else." As he spoke Mack tried his damnedest not to stare at the way the soft red material of her dress hugged every loving inch of her body. The way he was dying to do.

She shrugged. "No, I'm not exp—uh, no. Come in."

He blew out a breath of relief, then waited until she'd closed the door before taking her in his arms.

He lowered his head slowly, giving her a chance to push him away. When she didn't, he brought his mouth down on hers for a deep, erotic kiss that left them both gasping for air.

"My God, Becky. You are the most beautiful woman I have ever seen."

She smiled shyly, and he wondered if it was possible she really didn't know how gorgeous she looked.

"Do you honestly think so?" she asked, brushing her hair out of her eyes with a trembling hand.

He gave her a doubtful look, then smiled. "You're not calling me a liar again, are you?"

She bit her bottom lip. "No."

"Good, because I've turned over a new leaf—no more lies. Or deceptions," he added, certain she would understand he was referring to his father without him having to spell it out. She'd always seemed to understand the important things without him having to tell her.

She nodded knowingly, confirming his belief, then pulled his head down for another kiss. "I missed you so."

"I missed you too." He drew her closer, squeezing her so tight, he scrunched the paper sack against her back.

She twisted her head over her shoulder, trying to see what he'd brought with him. "Is that a present for me?"

"No! I mean . . . yes. Maybe. Later, that is." Completely flustered, he let go of her and rushed into the kitchen to set the bag on the table, then hurried back to her side.

Now that he was there, however—and had broken the ice, so to speak—he didn't know how to begin.

"Would you like to sit down?" she asked.

He looked around, then shook his head. "Uh, no. I think it might be better if I stand."

"Why's that?"

"Because I have some things I want to say to you, and I'm afraid of how you might react."

"Afraid?" Becky's heart melted when he gazed at her with uncertainty. She stepped back into his embrace and wrapped her arms around his neck. "You don't ever have to be afraid of me, Mack."

"Oh, I don't know about that. You pack a pretty mean punch, Miss de Bieren. Or at least your purse does."

Laughing, she gave him a gentle tap on his noggin. "Since when did the cynical Detective Hoyle develop such a keen sense of humor?"

He gazed down at her, no longer smiling. "Since a particular ray of sunshine about this big"—he held one hand over her head—"walked into my life."

"Oh, Mack. That is the sweetest thing you've ever said to me." Becky felt tears well up in her eyes.

"Ah, come on, Becky. Don't do that." He used his thumb to wipe away a tear that had fallen, then kissed the damp path that trailed down her cheek.

She laughed at his obvious discomfort, but that didn't stop her tears. "I know it seems like I'm always crying, but I can't help it. I'm emotional."

He hugged her, stroking his hand over her hair. "Don't worry, I'll get used to it."

She leaned back in his arms, searching his eyes for some indication that this was another of his attempts at humor, but he didn't appear to be joking. "You will?"

"If you'll let me," he answered. "I really botched things up between us, Beck, but I think I know why, and I was hoping you would give me a chance to explain."

"Go ahead," she said, smiling because she sensed this would be difficult for him to talk about, and she wanted to make it as easy as she could for him.

He looked into her eyes. "At first I thought I was doing you a favor by letting you go. You already had your parents to worry about, and I didn't think you needed to worry about me getting hurt or whatever. But then I realized that it wasn't you I was thinking about—it was me. I was scared."

He took a deep breath before he continued. "For six years I've been terrified that if I got seriously involved with a woman, I could someday end up like my father, lying flat on my back, wasting away, dependant on my wife to take care of me. I just couldn't face it. So I avoided entanglements."

"And when I came along and you found me irresistible," she said, trying to add some levity when she suspected he needed it most, "you pulled your Big Bad Wolf routine on me and tried to scare me away."

"I did my damnedest."

"Well, now you know, Mr. Wolf—I don't scare easily."

He chuckled. "Isn't that the truth."

"I'll always be there for you, Mack. You know that, don't you. No matter what happens, I'll be strong. And I know I must have looked like I was running away from the situation when you took me up to your father's room—"

"No. You were running away from me. I was such a bastard to you that night. I don't blame you for wanting to get as far away from me as possible. Can you forgive me?"

Becky wondered if she could ever love him more than she did at that moment. "I already have."

He gave her another long kiss. "You're the strongest woman I know—next to my mother, that is. She was partly responsible for me seeing how wrong I've been about this."

"Have you talked to her since—"

"I made an ass of myself the other night. Yes. I just came from her house. I apologized, and I told her she made me understand that it was worse to go through life alone—without someone to depend on being there for you—than it was to take a risk that you both might have to go through hard times someday . . . together."

Becky felt another tear slide down her cheek. "That must have made her very happy."

"You can say that again. But she wasn't the only one who helped me see what was important here. You did too. Because I thought about how good it had felt to come home with you after I was released from the hospital, how wonderful it was to have someone to talk to, to hold me, make love to," he added, smiling sweetly. "You listened to me pour out my frustrations about the way the operation got messed up. You held my hand when I told you how bad I felt about having to shoot that kid. I never knew how much I needed someone—how good it would feel to have someone—until I met you. You're my anchor, Beck. I love you and I don't want to live without you."

"Oh, Mack." She reached up and brushed that errant lock of hair off his forehead, her fingers grazing over the tiny scar left by the rock-throwing incident the day they'd met. "I love you too."

He sighed, letting go of the tension that had been penned up inside of him for days. "You're a very special woman, Beck, and I'm glad I found you."

She leaned back in his arms and gazed up at him with love in her eyes. "Woman? You don't think I'm a . . . well, little girl?"

He released her and stood back, taking in his fill of her from the top of her head to the tip of her toes, shaking his head all the while.

"No way. Not in that dress. Not out of it either," he said, wiggling his brows suggestively. "Don't forget—I know what you're like in the bedroom, Little Red Riding Hood."

Becky felt herself blush. "Oh, Mack . . ."

He tipped his head back and roared with laughter. Taking her hand, he started down the hall toward her bedroom. "Come with me, little girl. I'll show you what I mean when I say *woman*."

She trailed along behind him willingly, knowing they were in for one very special night.

Once in the bedroom, he stood her by the side of the bed. "Sit down. I'll be right back." A moment later, he returned with the paper sack he'd set on the kitchen table and handed it to her.

"What's this?" she said, starting to open the bag. He stopped her by putting his hands over hers.

"Wait. There's something I have to say first. These last few days when I was trying to stay away from you, I knew it was hurting you, but I kept telling myself it was for your protection. Then I realized that when I was with you, I never gave protection a thought. I'm sorry, and"—he broke out in a big smile—"I sure hope you're still in a forgiving mood, because I brought plenty of protection this time." He let her hands go.

Puzzled, she upended the bag. A half-dozen boxes of condoms fell out onto the bed. Her eyes widened, then she pursed her lips into a grim expression.

"Why you—you came here thinking you were going to—"

Seeing she was getting ready to work herself into another emotional tizzy, Mack dove onto the bed and pulled her into his arms.

"Now, don't go jumping to conclusions. I just wanted to be prepared in case you forgave me, that's all." He trapped her beneath him, using one leg to hold her squirming body still. His eyes filled with love and desire, he lowered his head to kiss her, the deepest, most sensuous kiss he'd ever given her. "Have you?"

Dazed by his kiss, she stared up at him. "Have I what?"

"Forgiven me."

"Well . . . I suppose." She pushed his jacket off his shoulders, then started unbuttoning his shirt. "But Mack—*six* boxes of condoms? Isn't that a bit much?"

He shook his head as he slid the sleeves of her dress down over her shoulders, exposing her breasts. "I'm learning to be optimistic."

"Finally," she said with a huge grin.

"And besides." He drew one nipple into his mouth and sucked it into a hard point. "I didn't know which kind you preferred, and a very wise lady told me that women like to make their own decisions these days."

"We do, but there's just one problem."

He lifted his head. "What's that?"

"I decided I want a big family," she replied, and swept all the boxes off the bed and onto the floor, well out of reach.

He lowered his head until his lips were a fraction of an inch from hers. "So, let's get started."

THE EDITOR'S CORNER

Next month, LOVESWEPT is proud to present **CONQUERING HEROES,** six men who know what they want and won't stop until they get it. Just when summer is really heating up, our six wonderful romances sizzle with bold seduction and daring promises of passion. You'll meet the heroes of your wildest fantasies who will risk everything in pursuit of the women they desire, and like our heroines, you'll learn that surrender comes easily when love conquers all.

The ever-popular Leanne Banks gives us the story of another member of the Pendleton family in **PLAYING WITH DYNAMITE,** LOVESWEPT #696. Brick Pendleton is stunned when Lisa Ransom makes love to him like a wild woman, then sends him away! He cares for her as he never has another woman, but he just can't give her the promise that she insists is her dearest dream. Lisa tries to forget him, ignore him, but he's gotten under her skin, claiming her with every caress of his mouth and hands. The fierce demolition expert knows everything about tearing things down, but rebuilding Lisa's trust means fighting old demons—and confessing fear. **PLAY-ING WITH DYNAMITE** is another explosive winner from Leanne.

CAPTAIN'S ORDERS, LOVESWEPT #697, is the newest sizzling romance from Susan Connell, with a hero you'll be more than happy to obey. When marina captain Rick Parrish gets home from vacation, the last thing he expects to find is his favorite hang-out turned into a fancy restaurant by Bryn Madison. The willowy redhead redesigning her grandfather's bar infuriates him with her plan to sell the jukebox and get rid of the parrot, but she stirs long-forgotten needs and touches him in dark and lonely places. Fascinated by the arrogant and impossibly handsome man who fights to hide the passion inside him, Bryn aches to unleash it. This determined angel has the power to heal his sorrow and capture his soul, but Rick has to face his ghosts before he can make her his forever. This heart-stopping romance is what you've come to expect from Susan Connell.

It's another powerful story of triumph from Judy Gill in **LOVING VOICES**, LOVESWEPT #698. Ken Ransom considers his life over, cursing the accident that has taken his sight, but when a velvety angel voice on the telephone entices him to listen and talk, he feels like a man again—and aches to know the woman whose warmth has lit a fire in his soul. Ingrid Bjornson makes him laugh, and makes him long to stroke her until she moans with pleasure, but he needs to persuade her to meet him face-to-face. Ingrid fears revealing her own lonely secret to the man whose courage is greater than her own, but he dares her to be reckless, to let him court her, cherish her, and awaken her deepest yearnings. Ken can't believe he's found the woman destined to fill his heart just when he has nothing to offer her, but now they must confront the pain that has drawn them together. Judy Gill will have you laughing and crying with this terrific love story.

Linda Warren invites you to get **DOWN AND DIRTY**, LOVESWEPT #699. When Jack Gibraltar refuses to help archeology professor Catherine Moore find her missing aunt, he doesn't expect her to trespass on his turf, looking for information in the seedy Mexican bar! He admires her persistence, but she is going to ruin a perfectly good con if she keeps asking questions . . . not to mention drive him crazy wondering what she'll taste like when he kisses her. When they are forced to play lovers to elude their pursuers, they pretend it's only a game—until he claims her mouth with sweet, savage need. Now she has to show her sexy outlaw that loving him is the adventure she craves most. **DOWN AND DIRTY** is Linda Warren at her best.

Jan Hudson's conquering hero is **ONE TOUGH TEXAN**, LOVESWEPT #700. Need Chisholm doesn't think his day could possibly get worse, but when a nearly naked woman appears in the doorway of his Ace in the Hole saloon, he cheers right up! On a scale of one to ten, Kate Miller is a twenty, with hair the color of a dark palomino and eyes that hold secrets worth uncovering, but before he can court her, he has to keep her from running away! With his rakish eye patch and desperado mustache, Need looks tough, dangerous, and utterly masculine, but Kate has never met a man who makes her feel safer—or wilder. Unwilling to endanger the man she loves, yet desperate to stop hiding from her shadowy past, she must find a way to trust the hero who'll follow her anywhere. **ONE TOUGH TEXAN** is vintage Jan Hudson.

And last, but never least, is **A BABY FOR DAISY**, LOVESWEPT #701, from Fayrene Preston. When Daisy Huntington suggests they make a baby together, Ben McGuire gazes at her with enough intensity to strip the varnish from the nightclub bar! Regretting her impulsive words almost immediately, Daisy wonders if the man might just be worth the challenge. But when she finds an abandoned baby in her car minutes later, then quickly realizes that several dangerous men are searching for the child, Ben becomes her only hope for escape! Something in his cool gray eyes makes her trust him—and the electricity between them is too delicious to deny. He wants her from the moment he sees her, hungers to touch her everywhere, but he has to convince her that what they have will endure. Fayrene has done it again with a romance you'll never forget.

Happy reading,

With warmest wishes,

Nita Taublib

Nita Taublib

Associate Publisher

P.S. There are exciting things happening here at Loveswept! Stay tuned for our gorgeous new look starting with our August 1994 books—on sale in July. More details to come next month.

P.P.S. Don't miss the exciting women's novels from Bantam that are coming your way in July—**MISTRESS** is the newest hardcover from *New York Times* best-selling author Amanda Quick; **WILDEST DREAMS,** by best-selling author Rosanne Bittner, is the epic, romantic saga of a young beauty and a rugged ex-soldier with the courage to face hardship and deprivation for the sake of their dreams; **DANGEROUS TO LOVE,** by award-winning Elizabeth Thornton, is a spectacular historical romance brimming with passion, humor, and adventure; **AMAZON LILY,** by Theresa Weir, is the classic love story in the best-selling tradition of *Romancing the Stone* that sizzles with passionate romance and adventure as deadly as the uncharted heart of the Amazon. We'll be giving you a sneak peek at these terrific books in next month's LOVESWEPTs. And immediately following this page look for a preview of the exciting romances from Bantam that are *available now*!

Don't miss these extraordinary books by
your favorite Bantam authors

On sale in May:

DARK JOURNEY
by Sandra Canfield

SOMETHING BORROWED, SOMETHING BLUE
by Jillian Karr

THE MOON RIDER
by Virginia Lynn

DARK JOURNEY
by Sandra Canfield

From the day Anna Ramey moved to Cook's Bay, Maine, with her dying husband—to the end of the summer when she discovers the price of forbidden passion in another man's arms, DARK JOURNEY is nothing less than electrifying. Affaire de Coeur *has already praised it as "emotionally moving and thoroughly fascinating," and* Rendezvous *calls it "A masterful work."*

Here is a look at this powerful novel . . .

"Jack and I haven't been lovers for years," Anna said, unable to believe she was being so frank. She'd never made this admission to anyone before. She blamed the numbness, which in part was culpable, but she also knew that the man sitting beside her had a way of making her want to share her thoughts and feelings.

Her statement in no way surprised Sloan. He'd suspected Jack's impotence was the reason there had been no houseful of children. He further suspected that the topic of discussion had something to do with what was troubling Anna, but he let her find her own way of telling him that.

"As time went on, I adjusted to that fact," Anna said finally. She thought of her lonely bed and of more lonely nights than she could count, and added, "One adjusts to what one has to."

Again Sloan said nothing, though he could painfully imagine the price she'd paid.

"I learned to live with celibacy," Anna said. "What I couldn't learn to live with was . . ."

Her voice faltered. The numbness that had claimed her partially receded, allowing a glimpse of her earlier anger to return.

Sloan saw the flash of anger. She was feeling, which was far healthier than not feeling, but again she was paying a dear price.

"What couldn't you live with, Anna?"

The query came so softly, so sweetly, that Anna had no choice but to respond. But, then, it would have taken little persuasion, for she wanted—no, needed!—to tell this man just how much she was hurting.

"All I wanted was an occasional touch, a hug, someone to hold my hand, some contact!" She had willed her voice to sound normal, but the anger had a will of its own. On some level she acknowledged that the anger felt good. "He won't touch me, and he won't let me touch him!"

Though a part of Sloan wanted to deck Jack Ramey for his insensitivity, another part of him understood. How could a man remember what it was like to make love to this woman, then touch her knowing that the touch must be limited because of his incapability?

"I reached for his hand, and he pulled it away." Anna's voice thickened. "Even when I begged him, he wouldn't let me touch him."

Sloan heard the hurt, the desolation of spirit, that lay behind her anger. No matter the circumstances, he couldn't imagine any man not responding to this woman's need. He couldn't imagine any man having the option. He himself had spent the better part of the morning trying to forget the gentle touch of her hand, and here she was pleading with her husband for what he—Sloan—would die to give her.

A part of Anna wanted to show Sloan the note crumpled in her pants pocket, but another part couldn't bring herself to do it. She couldn't believe that Jack was serious about wishing for death. He was depressed. Nothing more.

"What can I do to ease your pain?" Sloan asked, again so softly that his voice, like a log-fed fire, warmed Anna.

Take my hand. The words whispered in Anna's head, in her heart. They seemed as natural as the currents, the tides of the ocean, yet they shouldn't have.

Let me take your hand, Sloan thought, admitting that maybe his pain would be eased by that act. For pain was exactly what he felt at being near her and not being able to touch her. Dear God, when had touching her become so important? Ever since that morning's silken memories, came the reply.

What would he do if I took his hand?
What would she do if I took her hand?

The questions didn't wait for answers. As though each had no say in the matter, as though it had been ordained from the start, Sloan reached for Anna's hand even as she reached for his.

A hundred recognitions scrambled through two minds: warmth, Anna's softness, Sloan's strength, the smallness of Anna's hand, the largeness of Sloan's, the way Anna's fingers entwined with his as though clinging to him for dear life, the way Sloan's fingers tightened about hers as though he'd fight to the death to defend her.

What would it feel like to thread his fingers through her golden hair?

What would it feel like to palm his stubble-shaded cheek?

What would it feel like to trace the delicate curve of her neck?

What would it feel like to graze his lips with her fingertips?

Innocently, guiltily, Sloan's gaze met Anna's. They stared—at each other, at the truth boldly staring back at them.

With her wedding band glinting an ugly accusation, Anna slowly pulled her hand from Sloan's. She said nothing, though her fractured breath spoke volumes.

Sloan's breath was no steadier when he said, "I swear I never meant for this to happen."

Anna stood, Sloan stood, the world spun wildly. Anna took a step backward as though by doing so she could outdistance what she was feeling.

Sloan saw flight in her eyes. "Anna, wait. Let's talk."

But Anna didn't. She took another step, then another, and then, after one last look in Sloan's eyes, she turned and raced from the beach.

"Anna, please . . . Anna . . . *Ann-nna!*"

SOMETHING BORROWED, SOMETHING BLUE
by
Jillian Karr

When the "Comtesse" Monique D'Arcy decides to
feature four special weddings on the pages of her
floundering *Perfect Bride* magazine, the brides find
themselves on a collision course of violent passions
and dangerous desires.

*The T.V. movie rights for this stunning novel have
already been optioned to CBS.*

The intercom buzzed, braying intrusively into
the early morning silence of the office.

Standing by the window, looking down at the sea
of umbrellas bobbing far below, Monique D'Arcy
took another sip of her coffee, ignoring the insistent
drone, her secretary's attempt to draw her into the
formal start of this workday. Not yet, Linda. The
Sinutab hasn't kicked in. What the hell could be so
important at seven-thirty in the morning?

She closed her eyes and pressed the coffee
mug into the hollow between her brows, letting
the warmth seep into her aching sinuses. The
intercom buzzed on, relentless, five staccato blasts

that reverberated through Monique's head like a jackhammer.

"Dammit."

She tossed the fat, just-published June issue of *Perfect Bride* and a stack of next month's galleys aside to unearth the intercom buried somewhere on her marble desk. She pressed the button resignedly. "You win, Linda. What's up?"

"Hurricane warning."

"*What?*" Monique spun back toward the window and scanned the dull pewter skyline marred with rain clouds. Manhattan was getting soaked in a May downpour and her window shimmered with delicate crystal droplets, but no wind buffeted the panes. "Linda, what are you talking . . ."

"Shanna Ives," Linda hissed. "She's on her way up. Thought you'd like to know."

Adrenaline pumped into her brain, surging past the sinus headache as Monique dove into her fight or flee mode. She started pacing, her Maud Frizon heels digging into the plush vanilla carpet. Shanna was the last person in the world she wanted to tangle with this morning. She was still trying to come to grips with the June issue, with all that had happened. As she set the mug down amid the organized clutter of her desk, she realized her hands were shaking. Get a grip. Don't let that bitch get the better of you. *Oh, God, this is the last thing I need today.*

Her glance fell on the radiant faces of the three brides smiling out at her from the open pages of the magazine, faces that had haunted her since she'd found the first copies of the June issue in a box beside her desk a scant half hour earlier.

Grief tore at her. Oh, God, only three of us. There were supposed to have been four. There *should* have been four. Her heart cried out for the one who was missing.

This had all been her idea. Four stunning brides, the weddings of the year, showcased in dazzling style. Save the magazine, save my ass, make Richard happy. All of us famed celebrities—except for one.

Teri. She smiled, thinking of the first time she'd met the pretty little manicurist who'd been so peculiarly reluctant at first to be thrust into the limelight. Most women dreamed of the Cinderella chance she'd been offered, yet Teri had recoiled from it. *But I made it impossible for her to refuse. I never guessed where it would lead, or what it would do to her life.*

And Ana, Hollywood's darling, with that riot of red curls framing a delicate face, exuding sexy abandon. Monique had found Ana perhaps the most vulnerable and private of them all. *Poor, beautiful Ana, with her sad, ugly secrets—I never dreamed anyone could have as much to hide as I do.*

And then there was Eve—lovely, tigerish Eve, Monique's closest friend in the world, the once-lanky, unsure teenage beauty she had discovered and catapulted to international supermodel fame. *All I asked was one little favor . . .*

And me, Monique reflected with a bittersweet smile, staring at her own glamorous image alongside the other two brides. Unconsciously, she twisted the two-and-a-half-carat diamond on her finger. Monique D'Arcy, the Comtesse de Chevalier. *If only they knew the truth.*

Shanna Ives would be bursting through her door any minute, breathing fire. But Monique couldn't stop thinking about the three women whose lives had become so bound up with her own during the past months. Teri, Ana, Eve—all on the brink of living happily ever after with the men they loved . . .

For one of them the dream had turned into a nightmare. *You never know what life will spring on you*, Monique thought, sinking into her chair as the rain pelted more fiercely against the window. *You just never know. Not one of us could have guessed what would happen.*

She hadn't, that long-ago dawn when she'd first conceived the plan for salvaging the magazine, her job, and her future with Richard. Her brilliant plan. She'd had no idea of what she was getting all of them into. . . .

THE MOON RIDER

by VIRGINIA LYNN

bestselling author of
IN A ROGUE'S ARMS

"Lynn's novels shine with lively adventures,
a special brand of humor
and sizzling romance."
—*Romantic Times*

When a notorious highwayman accosted Rhianna and her father on a lonely country road, the evening ended in tragedy. Now, desperate for the funds to care for her bedridden father, Rhianna has hit upon an ingenious scheme: she too will take up a sword—and let the heartless highwayman take the blame for her robberies. But in the blackness of the night the Moon Rider waits, and soon this reckless beauty will find herself at his mercy, in his arms, and in the thrall of his raging passion.

"Stand and deliver," she heard the highwayman say as the coach door was jerked open. Rhianna gasped at the stark white apparition.

Keswick had not exaggerated. The highwayman was swathed in white from head to foot, and she thought at once of the childhood tales of ghosts that had made her shiver with delicious dread.

There was nothing delicious about this apparition.

A silk mask of snow-white was over his face, dark eyes seeming to burn like banked fires beneath the material. Only his mouth was partially visible, and he was repeating the order to stand and deliver. He stepped closer to the coach, his voice rough and impatient.

Llewellyn leaned forward into the light, and the masked highwayman checked his forward movement.

"We have no valuables," her father said boldly. Lantern light glittered along the slender length of the cane sword he held in one hand. "I demand that you go your own way and leave us in peace."

"Don't be a fool," the Moon Rider said harshly. "Put away your weapon, sir."

"I have never yielded to a coward, and only cowards hide behind a mask, you bloody knave." He gave a thrust of his sword. There was a loud clang of metal and the whisk of steel on steel before Llewellyn's sword went flying through the air.

For a moment, Rhianna thought the highwayman intended to run her father through with his drawn sword. Then he lowered it slightly. She studied him, trying to fix his image in her mind so that she could describe him to the sheriff.

A pistol was tucked into the belt he wore around a long coat of white wool. The night wind tugged at a cape billowing behind him. Boots of white leather fit him to the knee, and his snug breeches were streaked with mud. He should have been a laughable figure, but he exuded such fierce menace that Rhianna could find no jest in what she'd earlier thought an amusing hoax.

"Give me one reason why I should not kill you on the spot," the Moon Rider said softly.

Rhianna shivered. "Please sir—" Her voice quivered and she paused to steady it. "Please—my father means no harm. Let us pass."

"One must pay the toll to pass this road tonight, my lovely lady." He stepped closer, and Rhianna was reminded of the restless prowl of a panther she'd once seen. "What have you to pay me?"

Despite her father's angry growl, Rhianna quickly unfastened her pearl necklace and held it out. "This. Take it and go. It's all of worth that I have, little though it is."

The Moon Rider laughed softly. "Ah, you underestimate yourself, my lady fair." He reached out and took the necklace from her gloved hand, then grasped her fingers. When her father moved suddenly, he was checked by the pistol cocked and aimed at him.

"Do not be hasty, my friend," the highwayman mocked. "A blast of ball and powder is much messier than the clean slice of a sword. Rest easy. I do not intend to debauch your daughter." He pulled her slightly closer. "Though she is a very tempting morsel, I must admit."

"You swine," Llewellyn choked out. Rhianna was alarmed at his high color. She tugged her hand free of the Moon Rider's grasp.

"You have what you wanted, now go and leave us in peace," she said firmly. For a moment, she thought he would grab her again, but he stepped back.

"My thanks for the necklace."

"Take it to hell with you," Llewellyn snarled. Rhianna put a restraining hand on his arm. The Moon Rider only laughed, however, and reached out for his horse.

Rhianna's eyes widened. She hadn't noticed the horse, but now she saw that it was a magnificent Arabian. Sleek and muscled, the pure white beast was as superb an animal as she'd ever seen and she couldn't help a soft exclamation of admiration.

"Oh! He's beautiful. . . ."

The Moon Rider swung into his saddle and glanced back at her. "I salute your perception, my fair lady."

Rhianna watched, her fear fading as the highwayman swung his horse around and pounded off into the shadows. He was a vivid contrast to the darker shapes of trees and bushes, easily seen until he crested the hill. Then, to her amazement, with the full moon silvering the ground and making it almost shimmer with light, he seemed to vanish. She blinked. It couldn't be. He was a man, not a ghost.

One of the footmen gave a whimper of pure fear. She ignored it as she stared at the crest of the hill, waiting for she didn't know what.

Then she saw him, a faint outline barely visible. He'd paused and was looking back at the coach. Several heartbeats thudded past, then he was gone again, and she couldn't recall later if he'd actually ridden away or somehow just faded into nothing.

And don't miss these fabulous romances from
Bantam Books, on sale in June:

MISTRESS
Available in hardcover
by *The New York Times* bestselling author
Amanda Quick
"Amanda Quick is one of the most versatile
and talented authors of the last decade."
—*Romantic Times*

WILDEST DREAMS
by the nationally bestselling author
Rosanne Bittner
"This author writes a great adventurous
love story that you'll put on
your 'keeper' shelf."
—*Heartland Critiques*

DANGEROUS TO LOVE
by the highly acclaimed
Elizabeth Thornton
"A major, major talent . . . a superstar."
—*Romantic Times*

AMAZON LILY
by the incomparable
Theresa Weir
"Theresa Weir's writing is poignant,
passionate and powerful."
—*New York Times*
bestselling author Jayne Ann Krentz

OFFICIAL RULES

To enter the sweepstakes below carefully follow all instructions found elsewhere in this offer.

The **Winners Classic** will award prizes with the following approximate maximum values: 1 Grand Prize: $26,500 (or $25,000 cash alternate); 1 First Prize: $3,000; 5 Second Prizes: $400 each; 35 Third Prizes: $100 each; 1,000 Fourth Prizes: $7.50 each. Total maximum retail value of Winners Classic Sweepstakes is $42,500. Some presentations of this sweepstakes may contain individual entry numbers corresponding to one or more of the aforementioned prize levels. To determine the Winners, individual entry numbers will first be compared with the winning numbers preselected by computer. For winning numbers not returned, prizes will be awarded in random drawings from among all eligible entries received. Prize choices may be offered at various levels. If a winner chooses an automobile prize, all license and registration fees, taxes, destination charges and, other expenses not offered herein are the responsibility of the winner. If a winner chooses a trip, travel must be complete within one year from the time the prize is awarded. Minors must be accompanied by an adult. Travel companion(s) must also sign release of liability. Trips are subject to space and departure availability. Certain black-out dates may apply.

The following applies to the sweepstakes named above:

No purchase necessary. You can also enter the sweepstakes by sending your name and address to: P.O. Box 508, Gibbstown, N.J. 08027. Mail each entry separately. Sweepstakes begins 6/1/93. Entries must be received by 12/30/94. Not responsible for lost, late, damaged, misdirected, illegible or postage due mail. Mechanically reproduced entries are not eligible. All entries become property of the sponsor and will not be returned.

Prize Selection/Validations: Selection of winners will be conducted no later than 5:00 PM on January 28, 1995, by an independent judging organization whose decisions are final. Random drawings will be held at 1211 Avenue of the Americas, New York, N.Y. 10036. Entrants need not be present to win. Odds of winning are determined by total number of entries received. Circulation of this sweepstakes is estimated not to exceed 200 million. All prizes are guaranteed to be awarded and delivered to winners. Winners will be notified by mail and may be required to complete an affidavit of eligibility and release of liability which must be returned within 14 days of date on notification or alternate winners will be selected in a random drawing. Any prize notification letter or any prize returned to a participating sponsor, Bantam Doubleday Dell Publishing Group, Inc., its participating divisions or subsidiaries, or the independent judging organization as undeliverable will be awarded to an alternate winner. Prizes are not transferable. No substitution for prizes except as offered or as may be necessary due to unavailability, in which case a prize of equal or greater value will be awarded. Prizes will be awarded approximately 90 days after the drawing. All taxes are the sole responsibility of the winners. Entry constitutes permission (except where prohibited by law) to use winners' names, hometowns, and likenesses for publicity purposes without further or other compensation. Prizes won by minors will be awarded in the name of parent or legal guardian.

Participation: Sweepstakes open to residents of the United States and Canada, except for the province of Quebec. Sweepstakes sponsored by Bantam Doubleday Dell Publishing Group, Inc., (BDD), 1540 Broadway, New York, NY 10036. Versions of this sweepstakes with different graphics and prize choices will be offered in conjunction with various solicitations or promotions by different subsidiaries and divisions of BDD. Where applicable, winners will have their choice of any prize offered at level won. Employees of BDD, its divisions, subsidiaries, advertising agencies, independent judging organization, and their immediate family members are not eligible.

Canadian residents, in order to win, must first correctly answer a time limited arithmetical skill testing question. Void in Puerto Rico, Quebec and wherever prohibited or restricted by law. Subject to all federal, state, local and provincial laws and regulations. For a list of major prize winners (available after 1/29/95): send a self-addressed, stamped envelope entirely separate from your entry to: Sweepstakes Winners, P.O. Box 517, Gibbstown, NJ 08027. Requests must be received by 12/30/94. DO NOT SEND ANY OTHER CORRESPONDENCE TO THIS P.O. BOX.

SWP 7/93